"In MISCHIEF, Stefania Shaffer brings the world of Slater, Sibley and Ms. Burbank to life through vivid description and engaging dialogue. Characters become so real, readers can hear them interacting as Stefania masterfully weaves this tale. Cliffhangers abound, leaving readers unable to put down the book—salivating for the next in the series."

—*Daina Lujan, Principal, Millbrae School District; Vice President, South San Francisco Unified School District Board of Trustees*

"I highly recommend Stefania Shaffer's hilarious middle-grade novel, MISCHIEF, featuring daredevil Slater Hannigan and his crazy misadventures and perilous pranks. It's not only a fun ride with fresh characters for young readers—the author's underlying message of heart is relatable to all. I expect it to be a wonderful success and look forward to more from Ms. Shaffer."

—*Penny Warner, best-selling author of over 60 books for adults and children, including the Agatha Award winning middle-grade mystery series, THE CODE BUSTERS CLUB*

"MISCHIEF enables us to remember what it's like to be a kid, especially as it relates to boyhood. Her book gives insight for teachers into the world of the fifth grade mind and shows the heart and dedication required to teach, especially in times of struggle. Anyone involved in education, be it teacher, parent, grandparent or student will find MISCHIEF relatable, funny and engaging."

—Evona Mozulay Panycia,
Science Educator, Middle School and College Level,
Bernards Township School District and
Fairleigh Dickinson University, Madison, NJ

"Inspiring and heart-rending, MISCHIEF captures the essence of that student who does not yet believe in his own potential. Beyond the pulse-racing plot, readers will be turning pages at a clip to root for Slater Hannigan, hoping he learns the most worthwhile lesson of all—empathy."

—Audrey Fairchild, English Language Arts Educator, Ph.D
Hillsborough City School District

Mischief

BOOK 1

Book design by:
Arbor Services, Inc.
www.arborservices.co/

Printed in the United States of America

Mischief
Stefania Shaffer
www.StefaniaShaffer.com

1. Title 2. Author 3. Fiction

Library of Congress Control Number: 2017940735
ISBN 13: 978-0-9772325-1-2

Mischief

—— BOOK 1 ——

Stefania Shaffer

"There are only two kinds of children in the classroom: those who are at the center of trouble and those who are on the sidelines watching it brew."

—Madame Elsa Wilson, retired teacher, 5th grade,
Esther Bookman Elementary

For all of my twenty-seven hundred former students who are now teachers with their own class, or married, in college, or high school, I carry with me only the fondest memories of our time together. I never taught a student I believed would ever fail—childhood is meant for *learning.*
This book is for you. *—Stefania Shaffer*

Mis-chief: playful misbehavior or troublemaking, especially in children

Acknowledgments

Throughout my writing career, sturdy friends have offered me as much support as anything I might depend upon if I were adrift on a raft at sea.

My first readers outside of my home are these reliable logs that help me stay afloat, ensuring my foundation is set for the voyage ahead: Jenene Nicholson, Kathy Nelson, Cheryl Tyler, and Daina Lujan. Thank you for always finding the right *words* to say and the right *way* to say them. My writer's heart is always safe in your hands.

For the ties that bind and buoy me, I thank Joyce Walter, Erin Tolbert, Evona Panycia, Penny Warner, Judy King, Patti Smith, Maria Ribera, Martha Sutton, Fran Platt, Pam Kefer, Bronia Whipp, Heather McLean, and Heather Polcik for your moral support. Losing oars in the water is bad, but hearing encouraging cheers from the shoreline to *keep paddling by hand* is always good.

The compass is never wrong. Thank you to my enthusiastic beta readers for providing the navigation I needed when the last draft was complete. From former students to children across the country who read Mischief first, your special suggestions are etched within these pages.

For holding the binoculars to my work, I thank these San Francisco Bay Area professionals for consulting on fires, and juvenile law: Administrative Fire Battalion Chief, Kent Thrasher, Management Analyst, Matt Lucett, Police Captain, Patrick Halleran, Retired Assistant District Attorney, Robert H. Perez and Retired District Attorney, Jim Fox.

To my harbormasters, I thank my district of professional administrators and Board of Trustees for granting me this time to voyage, and for keeping the path home lighted. Dr. Maggie MacIsaac, Dennis Hills, Pam Scott, Vikki Ouye, Mark Intrieri, Kay Coskey, Davina Drabkin, Florence Wong, and Doug Luftman.

For my North Star, I thank the family and, especially, my sweet husband for supporting all of my dreams. You are my eternal reassurance and have been a constant bright source on this journey.

Without life preservers in publishing, one would be dead in the water. I am so grateful to the entire Arbor team, my editor Pam Nordberg and designer Rick Chappell. Your excellent work has readied Mischief to set sail.

Contents

CHAPTER 1

Last Days of Summer

"Boys, Gretchen is on her way," Lynn Hannigan hollers up the stairs. "Do you hear me?"

One more flight of stairs this morning reminds her she never should have bought this house with the staircase she never liked, the kitchen she did not want, and the garage apartment she did not need. But, the boys fell in love with the banister at first slide, and her husband's persuasive nature convinced her this would become the dream home she always envisioned. He is right about everything else except this staircase.

"Mom's calling us; hide the rope," Graham says to his older brother. He shimmies away from the door where his face has been perched sideways on the floor, looking from beneath the crack to keep watch for their mother's feet.

The doorknob turns in haste as Lynn pushes through, holding a

1

laundry basket of rumpled clothes fresh from the dryer. "Boys, I know you heard me calling you from downstairs. What do I say when I have to call you twice?"

Graham knows. He's heard it a million times. "Mom doesn't like to repeat herself. If Mom has to come up the stairs to deliver a message, then we aren't getting a second hour with our video games."

"Oh, Graham, I knew I did something right raising you," she says, putting down the basket and taking in Slater's room from corner to corner with her eagle eyes. It looks exactly as she expects. The rumpled bed sheets from the night before have been tucked in between the mattress and box springs the way she taught him to do before he sets foot out of his room. The rest of his things are put away, but his trophy case needs a dusting. The pollen blowing in from the trees outside will require Gretchen, their nanny, to do a little extra work today.

"Slater, I need to run an errand before the ladies arrive for the back-to-school mother's tea. Gretchen will be here shortly. I want you both downstairs, teeth brushed, hair combed, and fully dressed before she arrives," she says, her eyes fixated on the boys.

"Well, if the moms are coming here, can we go to Tobey's?" Slater asks, imagining their afternoon hijinks.

"When your father gets home from his golf game, he's taking you to the barber."

"What? No way. You said I could grow my hair like a hippie and you didn't care."

There it is, that tone that induces a calm, slithering smile across his mother's lips right before Slater realizes he is going to regret this.

"Oh, but Slater, that was meant to be for summer only. I am thinking a crew cut for the first day, the same kind they give in the military. Nice for a change, don't you think?"

He starts to open his mouth, but closes it quickly. The sooner she leaves, the sooner his plan can be carried out.

Glancing around the room one more time, she descends down the stairs for the dress shop four miles away.

"I'll be back in a little while." She lobs one last good-bye loud enough to carry her voice up to their room, and with purse in hand, the door clicks behind her.

"Oh, you're gonna be bald for the first day of school," Graham starts singing.

"You can laugh all you want, but I'm pretty sure Mom's getting us matching haircuts, so you're gonna be bald too," Slater says, jumping on Graham for a full-bore tackle to the floor. Even with plush carpet, a few rug burns will remind them of this wrestling match tomorrow.

The engine revs hard before they hear the squeal of gears grinding into reverse, then quickly into first. This signals to Slater and Graham that it is now safe to peek through their shutters, still half closed to block out the bright morning sun. When they spy her taillights turning the corner, they count the ten Mississippis it will take for her to realize she has forgotten something. When they see no sign of their mother's turnaround, Slater and Graham know she's really gone.

"Quick, pull out the rope, get the football helmets and the ice hockey pants. We probably have less than ten minutes." Slater barks orders while Graham digs through drawers of dressers to find the pads that belong inside the pants for extra protection when hitting the ice. They urgently race down the steps, grabbing at each other, the tangled rope trailing and dodging behind them. They need to slip out and get back before anyone knows they've even been gone.

Pajamas are tossed in a huddle of clothes already waiting to be sorted by Gretchen. Knee pads are hurriedly stuffed into the internal pockets of the hockey pants that fit them better a year ago when they were on the Wildcats. Helmets they used at this summer's football camp go on over tussled hair while mouth guards dangle from the frame along their chins.

"What if we break our arms? I don't want to start school Monday with another broken arm like last year," Graham says cautiously.

He remembers how bad Slater felt after they lost that chicken fight on the monkey bars. Who was to blame when Graham missed the next bar and fell backward off of Slater's shoulders? Slater was still racing ahead to beat the other players passing him to get to the opposite side. Graham could hardly remember the fall, or the crack of the bone that the other kids said made a sound like a whip. He was in and out of consciousness through most of the ride to the hospital in the librarian's minivan. Hers was the only employee car big enough to accommodate the school's stretcher, and since the hospital was nearby, it seemed like the most practical plan.

The part Graham remembers most about that day is how the doctors cut off his new Super Bowl jersey his dad brought home from the game played in Dallas. The pain was nothing compared to seeing the jagged fabric edges sliced up the middle, now a worthless souvenir. The other part Graham will never forget is how sorry Slater kept saying he was for racing faster than Graham's arms could latch on to the next bar. It was entirely his older brother's fault—they both knew it.

The itchy cast smelled worse than a wet sock loaded with rotting garbage. When the doctor sawed the cast off after Graham sweat through the entire month of September and most of October, it had the same kind of stink that comes from the back of the grocery store with all of the rotting fruit and old vegetables. Ah yes, the smell of rancid produce is only but a small obstacle to the great foragers on a quest to find the biggest boxes in existence. There are plenty of reasons to keep young boys entertained in the back lot of grocery stores, especially when it comes time to compete for who can make the biggest fort out of old cardboard. Even though Graham continues to play sports, the coaches all say he holds himself back on account of his fear of breaking that arm all over again.

"I know. Quick, wrap the pajama pants around your elbows and we'll wear our ski coats. That's all we need," Slater says so assuredly.

"But it's hot out. I don't want to sweat to death in this heat with my ski coat."

"Graham, you big baby, I should just leave you here. Put on the coat so you don't break your arm, and hurry, we have to go now if we don't want to get caught."

Always willing to go along with one of Slater's plans, Graham wraps his wild horses–patterned pajama pants around his elbow like a big gauze bandage. Even though it slips a bit, this will be better than nothing. He zips up his yellow down jacket and moves awkwardly to where Slater is maneuvering both of their skateboards.

"Hold these together, tight like this. First I'm gonna wrap this duct tape around both of the seats so they don't come apart when we're lying on them. Then we're gonna wrap the rope around them for extra security. It'll be like our raft when we go sailing down Parker Hill."

Slater is so confident about his plan. Hardly anyone is awake this early on a Sunday, so there's probably not even one car to worry about coming up the hill.

He and Graham slide out through the side door, do a double check up and down the street to make sure Gretchen's silver SUV isn't pulling up to the house yet, and when the coast is clear, they run.

"Graham, come on, faster! We've got to get to the other side of the school grounds and down the hill before Mom gets back. Hurry!"

"I'm hot. We should have put these jackets on after we stopped running," Graham shouts, panting. He rests his hands on his knees only for a moment before starting up again.

Parker Hill Boulevard—the longest and steepest hill in the neighborhood—has stymied many a cyclist after bragging how fast he could make it to the bottom without crashing. Some have reached speeds of 45 mph, which is faster than what cars are allowed to travel in this neighborhood. The police have already put in two stop signs to slow the traffic heading downhill, especially for the reckless drivers who keep plowing into Mrs. McGroover's garden wall made of stones.

Both skateboards have been thoroughly thatched together with duct tape and jump rope. Side by side is just enough width to provide Slater a cushy backseat, while he wraps his legs around his younger brother for protection. *Whose* protection is not quite clear.

"When I say go, we push off with our hands. Did you bring Dad's gardening gloves?"

"You never told me to," Graham says worriedly.

"Well, forget it; too late now. If we scrape our knuckles, that'll be the worst of it," he says with conviction.

Slater has never considered that anything bad will ever happen to him. He's lived a charmed life so far: baby model at two, commercials at six, Little League hitter at eight, fifth-grader next week.

With Graham cradled in his lap, the brothers lean against each other, their heads pointing back to slalom down Parker Hill Boulevard.

"Ready, set, go!" They push off from the pavement where their double-wide skateboard is smack center in the street facing the downward slope that would be at least a level three ski run if it had any snow.

"Ahhhhrg!" Graham screams for the length of six houses.

"I smell bacon!" Slater shouts above the sound of the whirring wheels that magically career past potholes that would have otherwise catapulted the brothers into a crumpled mess.

At a pace faster than they would ever be able to roller skate, they have caught enough momentum to sail uncontrollably with the weight of their two bodies carrying them forward like bullets dislodged from the chamber.

"How do we turn?" Graham shouts backward in a panic to his brother.

"I dunno. Get ready to ditch! On my count." Slater reels off his next command. But his voice cracks, giving way that instead of being in charge, he is now completely frantic.

Before they realize the worst part of this plan, they brace themselves for the crash that is coming up fast. Slater sees the truck in front of them. Its moving parts are standing still, parked along the curb with the wheels turned out. There is no time to count to three, no time to ditch. There is not even a second to brace for impact before the brothers collide into Mr. Turner's tire, knocking the wind out of them and dotting the road with their yellow coats and purple hockey pants.

Breathing deeply and slowly, this reminds Slater exactly how he felt the time he fell from the tree house four feet up. He landed on the grass then much harder than he thought dirt would feel. It was even worse than the belly flop he did in the pool during the end-of-the-year fourth grade celebration at Ben's house when he meant to do a dive like in the Olympics. Somewhere in the middle of his jackknife, he tried to somersault but hit the chlorine water like it was a cement bath.

"Graham, you good?" he asks without getting up yet.

No response. Slowly rolling over, he spies his younger brother facing flat on the asphalt. Graham's arms are pitched forward above his head, his body convulsing in quick movements. Where the yellow ski jacket has shredded in patches, its feathers fly about slowly in the breeze of the August morning air, whirring in a circle instead of falling to the ground.

"Graham, I'm coming," Slater says as he sits up slowly, seeing for the first time the pink flesh exposed on his knuckles and the crumbles of dark pavement bits ground into his palms.

Slater crawls three feet to where Graham is splayed out on the street. "Graham, you okay? Are you crying?"

He sees the look in Graham's eyes. It's the same expression his brother had last year when Slater took him on his first upside-down roller coaster since Graham was finally tall enough to ride. Graham was scared out of his mind then, which meant crying and grinning all at the same time.

"Mom's gonna be so mad," Graham says shakily. "I tore my coat." His eyes glisten while wet globs of snot hang above that mischievous grin behind his helmet.

"Dude, I did not see that coming," Slater says finally, laughing hysterically. He rolls on the ground, holding his knees tucked beneath him and then outstretching them wildly in a rhythm he and Graham repeat until they decide to inspect the tire treads in Mr. Turner's monster work truck.

"Good thing we didn't hit Mrs. Turner's car instead," Graham says.

"Oh, man, if we'd a hit that thing, you'd be a goner for sure," Slater throws back while caressing the tire that stands at eye level. "Her little putt-putt would be totally munched right now."

"Yeah, with my forehead buried inside her engine," Graham says eagerly.

"No, her engine's in the back. Your head would be buried inside her trunk!"

"Yeah, and parts of my face would be dangling all over the bumper where my teeth would be sitting right after they got knocked out," Graham continues with the ridiculous accounting of the adventure that could have been.

"Yeah, and your hair would be sliced off like an old bald guy's with just a flapping patch. It'd be like your toupee." Slater laughs until he has tears streaming down his face.

"Good thing I had on my helmet," Graham offers as his way of complimenting Slater on a detail well planned. "How long you think we been gone?"

"I dunno, but we better grab the boards and go." Slater surveys the scene. Not a scratch on Mr. Turner's truck. Not a soul stirring in the neighborhood. Not even a sign of curtains faintly moving in the front room windows, spying on what the Hannigan boys are doing out so early on a Sunday.

Their mother's friends are usually the first to call whenever a siren blares through the blocks where they live. "Hi, Lynn, how are you? Do you hear those sirens? Are the boys home?" As if their mother would ever say anything to give them up to the neighbors. She will only ever say, "Why, Liz, I thought those trucks were turning down *your* street." It would not matter that her boys are nowhere in sight. Their mother knows how to put up a good family front. She is cool that way. "Hannigans help ourselves" becomes the family motto.

Maybe he said it wrong. One of the kids' moms tried to correct Slater. "Hannigans help *each other*, you mean," she said, screwing up her face into a question mark, her squinty eyes peering beneath her downward-pointing brows, her lips curved upward into a side tilt. But Slater's pretty sure his mom means it the way she says it: "Hannigans help *ourselves*."

"I'm taking off this stupid coat, it's hot out here," Graham whines as he struggles to free himself of his skiwear and football helmet. He ties his horse pajama pants around his waist and trudges up the hill. The climb past ten houses will only get them halfway home. Then they need to trek through the school grounds and slip into their garage through the side door. The matter of combing their hair, brushing their teeth, and getting dressed is still a good fifteen minutes away.

"Glad you're okay," Slater says, bumping up against his brother and whipping him with the sleeves of his own ski jacket he is tying around his waist.

"That was cool," Graham shouts, walking backward up the hill, tossing his helmet at his brother. "You wanna do it again when we figure out a way to steer?" Slater offers with a gleam in his eye.

"What the heck is this?" In her front view, not even a quarter of a mile ahead, she sees two young boys high fiving each other and chest pumping. They also enjoy backward kicking each other in the butt while walking crookedly up the sidewalk of Parker Hill Boulevard. Carrying paraphernalia of a jump rope that twists behind them, sometimes used as a whip, loosely tied pajamas dangle from around waists, shimmying low on the hips. Football helmets are perched upon two bobbing heads, and lemon-colored coats with tiny feathers trail behind in a cocoon of goose-down dust.

"Hey, you boys need a ride?" she asks warmly. Finally, the best luck in the world. Gretchen, their nanny, pulls over and fills them with the juice shakes she just picked up for their breakfast.

Her fresh face and full-lipped smile are a welcome sight. She asks no questions because it's pretty obvious what this morning's adventure held. The only thing she can say is something they hear regularly from most of the adults they encounter. "What am I going to do with you?"

CHAPTER 2

First Day of School

Dana Burbank only has seven more wall displays to finish before she is ready to greet her new class of fifth graders. Toiling away on a Saturday when no one else is on campus is her favorite time to work. But, she has no idea that the peace and quiet she enjoys during these final days of summer will be disrupted shortly by a call from her principal. A highly coveted classroom is available, and surely Ms. Burbank will want to know. When she was a new teacher several years ago, she graciously agreed to occupy the long, dark portable near the sports field, across from the cafeteria. Awkwardly shaped like a rectangular trailer, its only benefit was that it came with manual air-conditioning. Mrs. Wilson's corner room will definitely be a trade up.

All of the new teachers wanted Room 14. The lottery draw went to Ann, but it took her only two minutes to take a polite pass once she saw how deep was the mess Elsa Wilson left behind buried inside every cupboard, closet, and drawer. Of course nobody ever expected a veteran teacher of forty years to empty those filing cabinets by herself. Still, Ann was never going to do the heavy lifting required to clear that jumble, so it would go to some other lucky teacher who wouldn't mind spending the entire summer doing room chores.

Elsa Wilson is one of the greatest teachers Esther Bookman Elementary has ever known, and that is what everyone kept saying with every toast over punch and cookies at her retirement party in June. She did have a magical way of managing her day. She used only a stony stare to put the fear into any child who ever merely *thought* of misbehaving in her class. Every now and then she would use her heft to slap her desk with both palms flat against the wooden surface to get the children's attention. This pronounced gesture alerted her students that an inspection of work was about to take place. One year she was rumored to have flipped the lid so forcefully on Jason Pierce's desktop that the entire contents inside spilled to the floor in a dramatic plunge, toppling the table along with it.

She only needed to build this reputation for herself in the early years of her teaching in order to enjoy a flawless routine for the rest of her career. Students knew what to expect—so did their parents. Every now and again came a hiccup in her system, but she had none of the problems that so many of the younger teachers experience with their rosters.

Fortunately, her time in education has been a delight. For most of her decades, she taught what she wanted and had little bother from anyone outside suggesting she do things differently. *Differently.* She always interpreted that word as becoming more *modern*, a term she despised. Yes, Elsa Wilson is finally ready to say good-bye. She has made some tremendous friends at Esther Bookman Elementary that she will keep. But, for now, she will enjoy what the world has to offer away from Room 14.

"Dana, hi, it's Bill Daly. You enjoying the rest of your summer off?" The principal's words catch her by surprise because the staff isn't due back for at least another week.

"Bill, how are you? Yes, yes, I'm great! Just great! Excited to be going back soon, can't wait," Dana says in her typically enthusiastic voice.

"Dana, I've got some news I think you'll be happy about," he offers genuinely. "Elsa's room is not going to Ann after all. Your name was on the next lottery ticket I drew, but I knew you were out of town for most of the summer seeing your family up north. Are you still interested in having a bigger classroom?"

"Oh, Bill, thank you so much! This is wonderful news! I haven't been in that room since I said good-bye to Elsa. I'm trying to remember now, how many walls are brick?" Dana asks, trying to mentally picture how many amazing displays she can create with the time she has left.

"Dana, I know Elsa left some files behind. Just get rid of whatever you don't want to keep and I'll have Al cart it away. Put it outside the room and we'll clear it out before Monday when the kids line up," he says with some relief.

"Perfect. I can work into next weekend to set up the room if I still need more time, no problem. Thanks again for the call and for the room, Bill. I'm going to be able to do lots of great teaching in that space," Dana says.

"Miss Burbank, there is no better teacher than you to reimagine an old space and make it sparkle. I can't wait to see how it turns out. Before I go, uh, Dana, there's something else I need." This is where the hesitation in his voice builds the tension on the other end of the phone.

Immediately suspicious that Room 14 is just a way to butter her up for whatever he needs now that he could not ask her about first, she starts in directly, "What is it, Bill?"

"Look, I need to make a change to your roster. I've got to add Slater Hannigan to your fifth grade. I know I promised that you wouldn't loop with him if you moved up from fourth grade, but honestly, we have a numbers issue and you already have a history with him," he says, stumbling his way through, bracing himself for her resistance.

"I can't believe it. I knew if I said yes to fifth grade you would put that kid back in my class. I trusted that you were going to put him with someone else. You cannot seriously think that this is a good idea or that he's going to even want to be back in my class. What about his mother? Have you told her?" Dana Burbank says, spitting tacks.

She dislikes Bill Daly because of his wishy-washy promises that never amount to anything.

"I haven't spoken with Mrs. Hannigan yet because I wanted to come to you first as a professional courtesy," Bill Daly says, looking at the string that has come loose from his pants where the top button now dangles in midair. "Look, Dana, I know you are a proud teacher and good with these energetic boys. Maybe it will just take one more year for a kid like Slater to feel like someone at school cares about him. I know *that* person is you," he says warmly.

"Energetic? I think it's more than that, Bill," she starts, impatiently. Right then, Miss Burbank is cut short by her boss's new words.

"Dana, I expect more from you. You're a leader at this school, and I know Slater Hannigan will not be the last challenging kid you will ever teach. Learn something from this experience that will make you stronger. Figure out a new way to interact with him. Will it help if we meet together with him and his mother before school on Monday?"

Obviously, with this decision made there is nothing more to say. He is her administrator, and she must comply. Last year was last year. New room, new attitude, maybe it will be this way for Slater Hannigan, too. But, if he's anything like he was last year, she will quit in October. She can always go back to her father's accounting firm and do people's taxes for the rest of her life. She will not waste another year playing tug-of-war with Slater Hannigan.

All of Dana Burbank's enthusiasm is drained from her. The renewed excitement she felt about her fresh start this fall has fizzled like the last balloon once the party ends. Deflated. That's the word. After spending the whole summer with her sisters and mother, all fellow teachers, venting about their year, she felt so much better. Certainly none of *them* had the rotten year she experienced. Yes, they were sympathetic. Sometimes they even tried to help her find the humor in some of Slater's antics. But, there were days when even they were flummoxed and never loved their own students more after hearing another one of her Slater stories.

In this moment, Miss Burbank is a child again when she telephones the only person sure to cheer her up. "Mom, it's going to be another horrible year," she says rapidly.

"What's this now? You were all excited to teach fifth grade; what's changed?" her mother asks.

"The principal just told me that Slater Hannigan will be in my class on Monday. I don't know why he's doing this to me. Wasn't last year enough?" Her voice shakes with frustration. She breathes quickly into a paper lunch sack—in and out the way she learned to do as a child before every gymnastic meet so she could calm herself in her corner before attacking her mat. If she forgets to breathe, she'll cry.

"In my early days, there was no such thing as a child who talked back to his teacher. All it took was one phone call home and that child's parent would dole out more punishment than cleaning chalkboard erasers after school for an hour would ever begin to impact," she continues with her memories from when Dana was a child eight presidencies ago.

"Mom, it's different now. He gets away with bloody murder because of his mother. He's not afraid of her at all since she doesn't ever think it's his fault," she says desperately.

"Dana, there are two things I know to be true about this situation. You are the adult. He is the child. It's really as simple as that. You hold all of the power. Do not let him think for a minute that he can rob you of any of it. You are the adult. You hold the power. Slater is a child," her mother says more forcefully than how she began.

Dana Burbank's mind turns over with last-minute remedies. She could just *not* show up on Monday, but then Slater Hannigan would know she was a coward. She could put in an application at any other school outside of the district. Even late hires can be good teachers—rarely, but it's happened. She could throw herself down a flight of stairs in her apartment building and stay home with a broken arm or two.

After she finishes her phone call, she repeats her mother's advice in a soft whisper to herself. "I am the adult. I hold the power. He is just a child. I am the adult. I hold the power." She says it evenly one hundred times, willing it to memory.

Room 14 is finally feeling less like Mrs. Wilson's learning center and more like Miss Burbank's academy for channeling potential. With every unrolling of the navy blue fadeless wallpaper stapled to the bulletin boards, her calm and confident demeanor returns. Yes, Ann was right to abandon this room. It has taken the better part of four days for Miss Burbank to haul out piles of old lesson plan files and any creative idea that may have been used, if only once.

There are puppets to support a history lesson on the important roles different presidents have played and how they are remembered. There are felt boards for every single state that one year's class created to make a life-size map standing as tall as any fifth grader. On it are details future classes were challenged to research about this state's government, origins, traditions, politics, indigenous birds, people, foods, culture, motto, and mood.

There are class sets of textbooks still dusty from twenty years earlier. Some are tucked in the way far back of one closet shelf. For decades, they would only be dug out on a substitute day for the one or two great stories that were never reprinted in the newer editions.

There are six other closets just like this. Overstuffed with volumes of workbooks used and graded and saved for last-day pass backs. Still, here they are abandoned with other newer workbooks from the year the publisher accidentally doubled the order.

When Al lays eyes on the heaping mound to cart away on the first day of school, he can only curse silently to himself the person who destroyed the order he created in his beautiful halls three weeks earlier.

"Good morning, class! Boys, can you hear me in the back? Line up!" Dana Burbank waits for her cluster of ten-year-olds to sort themselves into last name alpha order. Those who had her last year know this is usually a timed drill, but for today, she waits to see how long it takes them their first time. If she had a trumpet, now would be the time she would blare its horn. Instead, her referee's whistle seems like a feeble attempt in comparison.

The thrum of the ball has lodged itself inside the air passage, blocking the volume from sounding any louder than the hum of a reed against a clarinet player's lips. *Tweet, tweet,* her whistle calls shyly. She throws it back in her pocket and opts instead to use her PE voice.

"Boys! Turn around and face me now!" She has the attention of fourteen young ladies, all with eager smiles and new lunch boxes and backpacks. Miss Burbank has a reputation for order, and anyone who learned from her last year has already developed good study habits for life.

"Boys!" she says as she walks with her clipboard, checking off the names of those she recognizes from last year, making her way to the group huddled at the end.

"Hi, Miss Burbank," Tobey Peterson says coyly to alert the others that they are no longer alone. Another child not so innocent, but hardly the trouble that some of his best friends have become.

"Tobey, welcome back to school. Why aren't you boys in alphabetical order already?"

"We didn't know it was time yet," says Slater Hannigan.

"Good morning, Slater," she says, narrowing her eyes, hoping to convey to him the message that this year he is not getting away with his shenanigans. "Let's get you moved up to the middle of the line where the G through L kids are standing," she says patiently while preparing for his next misstep.

"What about them? They're not in line yet either," Slater says unabashedly, referring to the two classes on either side of Room 14's row.

"Slater, let's go. We're on the countdown now." Miss Burbank eyes the middle section where he is to be before the count of five. She doubles back to begin her head check from the front.

"Five, four . . ." Students hustle into a sloppy configuration nowhere near the correct spot that their last name would position them, "three, two . . ." Before she can finish, she is interrupted by the hush that comes over all of the grade level lines when Mr. Daly blows his bugle and Mr. Simon bangs his marching band drum.

"Esther Bookman students, good morning and welcome back to school," he says with a cheerful warmth. "Your teachers and I want you to know how happy we are to see you again. For those of you in kindergarten, we are excited to meet each of you and to assign you class buddies from Miss Thomlin's first grade and Mr. Simpson and Mr. Wallace's third grades.

"For our fifth graders, this will be a special year for you as you build your legacy project for this campus so we always have something to remember your time here," he says wistfully. "Last year's fifth graders were a model class, but I know how many leaders you have among you, and we are ready for the spirit and enthusiasm you bring to our campus." He looks up and down Miss Burbank's row.

"For all of you youngsters sandwiched into middle grades, we have a lot of fun field trips planned for your classes. So, everybody, have a great year. Teachers, let's get these students ready for class. Go, Badgers!"

The sorting that is nearly completed in Miss Burbank's line is in need of redoing. "Julia, you are an M. Let's move you away from Jennie Riggs. Franklin, you are not a P. Move up to stand behind Gary Lindstrom. Okay, everybody, starting at the head, I'm coming down the line. Stay exactly as straight as you are, and you will find your name plate and books on your desk as soon as you walk inside. Remember, when you cross the learning threshold, there should only be quiet with a two-inch voice," she says confidently as she moves quickly through the roster.

"Amy Adair, happy to see you. Jeff Brickman, it's going to be a good year. Daniel Adams, honey, go follow Amy." By the time five girls and five growing boys have shuffled past Miss Burbank, the class is not even halfway accounted. "Mitchell Gregory, hi, buddy. Slater Hannigan, let's make it a good year, Slater," Miss Burbank says loud enough only for Slater to hear. The rest of the class is seated, attendance has been sent along with the office aide, and Miss Burbank is ready to begin.

"I know many of you took some amazing trips this summer, and some of us enjoyed time with family at home. I want to share with you some of the memorable events that happened in our world this summer. Here is a look at what some remarkable children your age did around the globe." And with this the lights go off and the slide show begins.

"Macaroni. Macaroni," Slater whispers under his breath to

Macaroni, sitting two rows away. He rips out the last page of his own textbook, the one labeled "Index," and writes a note in Sharpie. "Tell them to do it at 8:49 a.m."

The plan that is already familiar to the others will occur exactly one minute from now. The scribbled note is ushered at a clip up and down the rows of the darkened room aglow only by the slide transitions. The music conceals the sounds of rushing as the elbows that have gained strength from pitching in Little League all summer are still adept at tossing balled papers across the room with a quick snap of the wrist.

Miss Burbank is pleasantly surprised by her first test at measuring attention span. She imagined there would be more unrest during the dimming of the lights, a trick she learned from Elsa Wilson. "Before lunch, dim the lights to see who is sneaking food from their backpack. After lunch, anytime you dim the lights, look to see who is sleeping and drooling on the desk. Any other time, look to see who is engaged and note taking," Elsa once told her while she feverishly wrote down all the advice this veteran had to share when Miss Burbank was a new teacher only six years ago.

The slides show other ten-year-old students from poverty-stricken neighborhoods in global villages where children are not allowed to go to school because they have to work in factories, fields, or fisheries. The images set to music dart between Cameroon, Nicaragua, and Haiti. Contrasting pictures of shattered glass on old school buildings that look half abandoned in American cities like Oakland, Watts, Chicago, and Detroit also appear. Wherever there is a family, there is a mother hoping for a way out for her child. Obviously, the point is supposed to be that education is not something to be taken for granted. Miss Burbank is certain her students will feel a wave of gratitude wash over them as each realizes *how lucky I am to be in Room 14 this year.*

Thud. Thwarp. Thwarp, thwarp, thwarp are the sounds of sharpened pencils being shot into the air at precisely 8:49 a.m. None of the sniggering can be contained, which signals the teacher to abruptly turn back on the lights.

"When we study our states this year, what surprises you most about the American cities you just saw in some of these slides?" Miss Burbank asks, hoping to engage the class with the level of empathy and care she would expect from global citizens.

Phil Moore can hardly keep a straight face, so he buries his head in his sleeve while resting his forehead on the desk. If he looks directly at Slater Hannigan, he is going to lose it completely.

"Phillip, what seems to be the trouble this morning?"

"No, it's nothing, Miss Burbank. I'm just so sad about all those little kids," he says so convincingly.

"It is sad, yes, but there is something we can do if we are to become globally aware of—" and before she completes her thought, her eyes give her away now. There, high above the heads of thirty students, are at least fifty pencils dangling from the ceiling tiles—thrust like spears into the panels of foam.

Quickly, Miss Burbank throws a look to Slater, who sits innocently

with his hands folded, eyes locked forward, doing nothing to indicate
he has the slightest clue as to what could be the matter.
You are the adult. You hold the power. Slater is a child, her
mother's voice repeats in her head.

Miss Burbank's inner voice is saying something else entirely.
Look away, and carry on as if there is nothing unusual, and so a
slow smile crosses her lips. She unfolds her arms from across her
chest and moves to sit atop her desk instead. After she crosses her
legs, Miss Burbank laces her fingers around the top of her knee
and sits up straight, flashing a steady gaze.

"Before we finish social studies this year, we will learn what our
founding fathers had in mind for the people of our country when
they built our Constitution. We are lucky that we have freedom
to pursue education. On this note, let's talk about expectations for
the year and the other areas we will be covering."

While Miss Burbank covers her long list of learning goals for
the year, Slater and Tobey are perplexed as to why this plan did
not get the rise they thought it would. "I-D-K," Slater writes on
a second Index page he has ripped out. He flashes it to Tobey in
the next row, where Macaroni can also see. He turns it over and
writes, "After lunch," which signals to them the quarterback has
called the next play.

CHAPTER 3

Barnyard Boys

"Oh, it's starting already. That Slater is up to no good," Miss Burbank says through bites of tuna salad stuffed into tomatoes she brought from her own garden. Her teacher friends are all surprised. They believed he would have at least made it through the first day with good behavior before they would be hearing tales of Slater and the drama that would befall this rascal.

"You know what you need to do, Dana? Start writing every single little thing down in a notebook and then call home," Miss Keaton states obviously.

"Jen, I will spend more hours of my day writing about Slater's antics and attitude than grading and making lesson plans. Plus, I can't just record suspicious behavior. I need to have proof—and all I have is nada and zilch, and they don't add up to much in court these days," Dana Burbank says, somewhat dejected.

"Dana, go ask Bill Daly if you can install a camera in your classroom," Miss Keaton says, determined to find a solution before the lunch recess bell rings in ten minutes.

"No way. He won't do it. We talked about that last year, and Slater's mother says it's against her son's constitutional rights to be videotaped all day." Miss Burbank vigorously recalls for the ladies the adamant tone Lynn Hannigan used to convey her point. "I feel like I am on the sharp end of a poking stick—that mother has got it out for me."

"Well, until the next time Slater Hannigan gets caught, I guess all you can do is teach the other students and hopefully he will go along with you and end up learning something useful this year," Miss Allie Carter says reasonably. She teaches kinders and has no clue about the little disasters she has sent forward. For all she knows, her students are eating their lunch from the cans of Play-Doh she never finds rolling around beneath her tables.

As Miss Carter folds the linen napkin she brings from home to put across her lap so she can feel like she is somewhere other than this third-rate teacher's lounge, everyone else hastily scooches between chairs, laughing wildly at the joke Chip Thatcher has just told.

"And that's why I said I'd rather be a baboon than an orangutan," he says dryly. His wife must be the luckiest girl in town because Chip Thatcher has one of the winningest personalities to ever grace this lunchroom. His students love him, especially when he's teaching them how to blow up something in science, or how to melt toy soldiers by using glass and the sun.

While the teachers mill around for a few more minutes, trusting that their students will be standing at the ready on their classroom line when the bell rings, Slater Hannigan and his friends have been making other plans to get a rise out of Miss Burbank today.

"She saw it, I know she saw it," Slater says insistently. As the other heads around his huddle bob up and down excitedly in agreement, they await words from their wise leader.

"What do we do, just let them dangle all day?" Tobey Peterson asks anxiously. "What if one of 'em falls and pokes out an eye? That'd probably be her fault because she wasn't doing such a good job of keepin' the room safe, right?"

Oh yeah. This gets them thinking about ways to shake the ceiling by throwing some of the rubber balls they are always buying from the quarter machine that also sells them their jawbreakers.

"No way. I'm dead if that ball hits a wall and ricochets back to Miss Burbank. Can't do it. I got in enough trouble last year. My mom said she's never been so embarrassed to be called to the principal's office as she was when I glued Miss Burbank's chair pillow to her skirt," Slater says, rolling backward and laughing uproariously at the memory of Miss Burbank awkwardly rising from her chair with a big cushion stuck to her butt.

At this retelling, the boys become engrossed in slapping each other's shoulders, dropping their hands to their knees and bending over with hysterics.

Yes, the laughter can be heard from across the courtyard where children have already been escorted inside Room 14, awaiting their lesson to begin. At once, Miss Burbank and her students all snap their necks toward the exit behind them. Through the door's view, they can see a cluster of boys rolling around the playground laughing at their own guffaws, hardly aware that the bell has already rung and no one else is outside.

Miss Burbank moves abruptly from her teaching circle as she crosses the room with enough gusto to make her skirt swish, a waft of tea rose perfume trailing behind her. "Boys, we are all waiting for you. The bell has already rung. Now you are tardy to class. And on the first day of school," she says, making her usual disapproving sound clucking her tongue behind her front teeth, "Tsk, tsk."

"Plan B, go to Plan B," Slater murmurs under his breath as the group rises from the ground and pulls each other up with one arm.

"I will expect a letter of apology before the end of the day," she says, somewhat pleased with herself. She knows this will be the first bit of evidence she will collect for Slater's file this year. The fact that it is from the first day of school is a gift. It will prove that Slater Hannigan's hooligan ways will never change.

During sustained silent reading time after lunch, Slater looks up from his book to see Phil Moore eyeing him from behind his own boring book. "When?" Phil mouths to Slater.

Slater positions his fingers inconspicuously at the spine of his book to count off three different numbers: two, zero, three. He is as fast as an umpire calling plays to the pitcher. His fingers glide quickly, and Phil reads the message loud and clear—at 2:03 p.m. Plan B will be in full force.

Phil makes sure to convey it to his row of students; however, he is not as sly because when he silently mouths the words, Miss Burbank thinks he is talking again.

"Phillip, what is it you would like to share with the rest of the class? Something interesting about your book, I hope."

"Um, Miss Burbank, I think I already read this book before. Can I get a new one from your library?"

"I suppose," she says, glad to see he is at least making an effort.

"Um, Miss Burbank, do you have a recommendation for me?" Phil throws that half smile with his blue eyes peeking from behind the swath of bangs hanging down to his nose.

"Slick. Way to get the teacher on your good side so early in the year, *Phillip*," Slater says in a mocking tone as Phil walks by Slater's desk to find *Anne of Green Gables* from Miss Burbank's bookshelf of her favorite classics. "*Phillip* got a girl book," Slater continues, chiding his friend.

"Don't worry, I'm not gonna read *this* one either," Phil says assuredly. "I don't care if I don't pass the reading test. Stupid quizzes, none of them even ask good questions."

"Boys, get back to your books, please. Reading time is over in another ten minutes," Miss Burbank says quietly.

The other kids are just as restless, so it takes only a few minutes for the room of wandering eyes to leave their pages and connect with Slater and Phil in knowing glances that confirm the secret agreement as to when Plan B will begin.

"All right, everybody. I have a new notebook here for each of you to write your thoughts and questions about today's reading. Keep this journal with your textbooks inside your desk so that I may look at it and record your progress."

"Can I have a green-covered notebook instead of blue, please?" Sibley White asks politely. She has a fabric theme covering all of her books, and her literature is always protected with some sort of green tree pattern, since paper makes books and paper comes from trees and trees are always green. Nobody likes Sibley.

"Here, Sibley, trade with Olivia. You don't mind do you, Olivia?" Miss Burbank is sure Olivia will be happy to oblige since Olivia is one of the most accommodating students Miss Burbank has ever taught. She was lucky enough to have her as a student last year, too.

While Sibley is stacking her color-coded, newly covered textbooks and workbooks inside her desk, Miss Burbank readies herself for the final lesson of the day, social studies.

"If you are on task and following today's agenda on the board, you can see it is time for history, so you should already have out your textbook, *We the People.* Place it on the top left corner of your desk and keep it closed until I finish introducing the lesson," she says without missing a beat.

Miss Burbank is glad the day is nearly over. With one hour to go before the dismissal bell will ring, this morning's minor crisis of fifty pencils dangling from the ceiling seems like so long ago. After an anxious night's sleep anticipating seeing Slater again, she has to admit, the day hasn't been as terrible as she feared.

"Who can tell me what our founding fathers really wanted when they were imagining a more perfect union?"

A few hands shoot into the air, but Olivia's wildly waving fingers signal the kind of enthusiasm Miss Burbank likes to see from her students. "Yes, Olivia, please answer."

"Our founding fathers imagined a more perfect union where everybody could have freedom to pursue whatever religion they wanted and they didn't have to pay all of the taxes that the king wanted them to pay to him, and they wanted to be able to have land to build their own homes and—"

"Hee-haw."

"Oink, oink."

"Cock-a-doodle-doo."

"Moo, mooo."

All at once, the classroom erupts into the sounds of a hundred barnyard animals. The hens are clucking. The roosters begin a crowing. The cows and the pigs are taking turns noisily competing against each other to be heard over the horses that are whinnying and the dogs that are barking.

"What on earth is happening here?" Miss Burbank shouts over her students who all look at her with a glimmer in their eyes. They can't *all* be in trouble if they are *all* in on the joke. She knows who is at the helm of this little game—Slater Hannigan, the world's greatest prankster.

The class cannot contain themselves. They are so pleased with their performance. Thirty ten-year-olds are all in cahoots at exactly 2:03

p.m. When does this ever happen without a lot of adult supervision? Plan B has come off without a hitch. This will surely go down in history at Esther Bookman Elementary as the greatest practical joke ever played on a teacher. Many of the girls go along with it because they know it will be hysterical; and yes, Sibley White participates because, of course, she is trying to make friends this year.

Miss Burbank is speechless. She has two simultaneous thoughts. One is *try not to laugh or this will never end.* The other is *Slater Hannigan is a child, I am the adult; he will not take my power.*

Suddenly, the class quiets down and becomes perfectly still just when the principal pokes his head in the doorway.

"Hello, fifth graders. Miss Burbank," he nods toward Dana Burbank, who is standing there red-faced. She has not had a chance to restore order before Mr. Daly makes his appearance during his afternoon rounds.

"Hello, Mr. Daly. The children were just playing a little practical joke," she says rather sheepishly, hoping his attention will not be drawn toward the ceiling tiles.

"It looks like Room 14 has had a rather eventful day." His eyes lock on the pencils that dangle above the heads of most children, except for one. How curious that Slater is safe from harm, seated exactly beneath the one tile that is free of any possible spears falling into his eyes.

"Yes, we have had our fun, but I assure you learning has taken place today. Why, we were just at the beginning of discussing the vision our founding fathers had imagined for our independence when the class became quite spirited," she says, hoping this is enough to convince Mr. Daly that she has this under control.

"Carry on, then," he says, scanning the room slowly until he gives Slater his last backward glance on his way out of the room. "What are you thinking, class? It's enough that you want to act like you are still in the fourth grade, but this is your final year of elementary and you are obligated to pass your standards tests if you plan to go to middle school next year. So I suggest you pull yourselves together, stop goofing off, and start focusing on what I am here to teach you." Dana Burbank is not smiling. In fact, she is starting to make some plans of her own. If this is how Slater Hannigan is willing to behave on the *first* day of school, it is going to be a long year ahead unless she can come up with a few surprises of her own for this child.

She eyes her students, slowly taking stock of the other culprits in Slater's ring. If she can pick them off one by one, then Slater will be left without an audience and maybe she will be able to get some teaching done this year.

Phillip Moore only transferred to this school last year. I'll have to check his student file in the office to see what circumstances made him leave his last school. Miss Burbank continues her calculation of Slater's friends. *Tobey Peterson stuck to Slater like glue last year at the Water Rapids Park. He's afraid to swim, but Slater shared all of his flotation noodles with Tobey. At least Mr. Daly had the good sense to keep most of Slater's sports friends in another class.*

"Miss Burbank?" Sibley White gently tries to get her teacher's attention. "Miss Burbank? Can I share what I think about what our founding fathers wanted for our country?"

"Yes, yes, of course, Sibley. Thank you." Miss Burbank takes her eyes off of Slater and sits on her teacher's stool. "Go right ahead." While Sibley recalls every plot point from her historical fiction American Girl series, Miss Burbank tries hard to ignore the thoughts she has about this class and what the year might bring. She hopes they can all have fun together the way she had with her students every other year. But she wants to have an easy time teaching and not have to worry so much whenever she has her back turned away from Slater and his buddies.

Ping, ping, shoop, plop. All it takes is one rubber ball sailing across the room to release eight pencil daggers from their ceiling tiles above.

Molly McCovey ducks just in time to avoid two spears piercing her eyeballs. Instead, they fall onto the back of her neck, landing softly in the ruching of her hoodie. However, she does not count on the ricochet of that ball returning smack dab into her face. Sadly, her slow reflexes do not prevent the lens from her glasses being knocked out of its frame. Thank goodness she is not blinded, but what will her mother say about replacing her new pair of glasses *again*?

While the walnut-sized yellow rubber ball falls to the ground and rolls faster than it can be captured, a green one is flicked into the ceiling even harder this time, taking six more pencils down with its first graze. Tobey catches it in midair and throws it to Slater, who catches it and quick releases it before Miss Burbank marches straight over to his desk.

"Give it to me now," she says with her arm extended and the palm of her hand facing upward.

Slater puts his palms on his tabletop, pushing unsuccessfully away since the metal frame of his chair is connected to his desk. "What? It wasn't me!"

"Slater, I am counting to three before I call Mr. Daly back in here. One." Miss Burbank hopes that Slater is going to do the right thing here because she doesn't want Mr. Daly to see what a mess this afternoon has become. "Two." She keeps her hand steady in front of Slater's face just waiting for him to put his little green ball into her clutches.

Smack. Slater slaps the palm of her hand with his own palm and then points his two fingers at her and says, "See, I've got nothing. I didn't do it!"

"Three," Dana Burbank says emphatically. She slowly turns away, her back facing Slater as she sighs deeply, dejected to know that she has lost this battle and must call the office for help against a ten-year-old.

As she reaches for the phone, a green ball comes sailing by her head, hitting the front bulletin board hard before its velocity changes direction and pings Delaney Shu right in the forehead. "Ouch," Delaney shouts as she rubs the pink welt forming above her eyes, trying to hold back her tears.

"Enough, boys! I've had it up to here with your welcome-back-to-school antics today. Let's see how you feel after serving detention this week in the cafeteria," Miss Burbank says with her voice low and her words coming out clearly one at a time between her clenched teeth.

"What did we do?" a chorus of wide-eyed innocent boys all in the back row and on the sides of the room bellow out in unison.

"I'm not serving no detention," Slater says in a huff. "It's not my fault you weren't watching the class good enough to see how those pencils got up there in the first place."

A hush comes over the room as anyone still snickering falls silent now. Slater just crossed the line. He has done it before, but this kind of confidence usually is not on full display the first day of school. The first day is to make sure the teacher doesn't learn your name. The first day is for just blending in. The first day is to see who all of the players are and to find the cool kids to befriend. No one as popular as Slater wants to do detention on the first day.

"Oh, my friend—I do not think you want to go down this road today," Miss Burbank says, eyeing him, tossing the ball in her hand after scooping it up from the floor on her way to his desk.

"You don't have any proof of anything anyway," Slater offers as a way to thwart whatever plans Miss Burbank thinks she has for him.

"Oh, don't I? Come with me." And with this Miss Burbank walks Slater next door to her buddy room for a time out with Mr. Wallace, the third-grade teacher famous for his collection of bow ties.

As she returns to Room 14, she throws a steely glare up and down the rows. "Class, silently pull out a sheet of binder paper." The perspiration in the room is detectable as a class of ten-year-olds sweats, even those who have no reason to feel guilty. "Write for me what you just witnessed this afternoon, and I expect you to be truthful. Sign your name, then turn it facedown when you are finished, and I will collect it in ten minutes," Dana Burbank says in a sharp tone.

Her students may not know her well yet, but they can tell she means business in this moment. Lying to a teacher at the beginning of the school year will only set you up for problems down the road, and nobody wants to be held back when their friends are going on to middle school. So not one single kid even thinks about bending the truth.

As Slater sits alone in Room 12 with a room full of eight-year-olds coloring maps of the United States, Miss Burbank's students all write testimony about how a little yellow ball started the unraveling of their first history lesson of the year—constitutional rights are only for those allowed to vote. Slater will soon find out who his real friends are and who his enemies will be for the rest of the year. He already knows Miss Burbank is out to get him.

By the time of his annual Halloween event spectacular, everyone in the whole school will be wishing for their own invitation, if it's anything like last year. But by the end of this fateful night, he will be unpopular with one more person.

CHAPTER 4

Halloween at Hannigans

"Slater." Lynn Hannigan greets her son with a familiar tone as soon as he walks through the front door.

"What, Mom?" he shoots back.

"Do not 'What, Mom?' me, Slater. I want to talk to you about a little email I received from Miss Burbank right after you left her classroom this afternoon."

"Mom, I didn't do it. She's always picking on me, and I can't help that she has no control over the situation unless it's stupid Constitutional stuff. So boring anyway. Who needs to know about stuff from a hundred years ago?"

"Slater, the fact that our country is going on two hundred and fifty years old is one more reason we need to get you a tutor. Settle down and come sit with me in the kitchen."

Lynn moves from the front door to the refrigerator to make Slater a treat. She grabs a carton of milk, a bag of frozen cherries, some spinach, and a banana to throw into her high-end blender. Presto! A healthy shake in one minute flat served in his favorite Knights of the Round Table silver goblet from when he was last at Disneyland two years ago. He is not into knights in shining armor anymore, but the mammoth-sized goblet is still pretty cool for getting bigger portions on everything he loves.

"Slater," Lynn Hannigan begins calmly, "what happened to our agreement this summer that you would be on your best behavior for Miss Burbank so that you could earn some of the privileges you want?"

"Mom, I swear, it wasn't me. What'd she tell you anyway?" he asks before he determines how much information he needs to give up.

"In her email, Miss Burbank said that there was some trouble at the beginning of the day with pencils dangling from her ceiling. Was this you?" She leans over to dab at his face with a napkin while Slater grabs it from her to finish wiping his own mouth with the back of his hand.

"Mom, I'm telling you for the last time, it wasn't me."

"Well, do you know anything about a rubber ball flying through the air to knock those pencils down?" His mother scoots her stool a bit closer to stroke his soft, brown hair the way she used to when it cupped his ears before it was newly shorn.

Her words are calm and inviting, a welcome mat for the truth to be laid in front of her feet. She is patient with Slater because she knows how hard last year was with Miss Burbank. She also knows what murder it was behind the scenes this summer to try and get him placed into anyone else's fifth-grade class. But, she knows now what to expect from Miss Burbank, and so does Slater. *If everyone can let go of last year, maybe there will be a chance for something really good to come from this year.* At least this was the point of view Principal Daly kept selling.

"Mom, stop touching me. I'm not a baby," Slater reels off, jumping down from his stool.

"Slater, of course you're not a baby, but I remember when you were and I can't believe how fast you are growing up," his mother says almost wistfully. She wants to hug him, but she can tell he is in one of his moods, so she only extends her arm across the kitchen island and pats the counter to indicate that he can sit back down for a little while longer and she will stay on her side of the blender.

"Slater, were you tardy to class after lunch?"

"Mom, I didn't hear the bell, or the whistle. I was hanging with my friends and we were just laughing. Miss Burbank acted like we were doing something bad, and we weren't, I swear."

"Slater, do you remember the talk we had about Dad and how he built his campaign on his reputation for doing the right thing?"

"I know it," Slater says with his head down, staring straight into the empty goblet he guzzled from five minutes ago.

"I don't think your father would be where he is today if he couldn't admit to his mistakes and if he couldn't build relationships with people who disagreed with him," she says warmly.

"Yeah, but Dad doesn't have a teacher who doesn't like him."

Slater pushes out the words with a gust of air, finally admitting something that he hopes will satisfy his mother and get her to leave him alone.

"Well, I will acknowledge, Slater, that you and Miss Burbank have had your differences, and as much as I will stick up for you in public, I do not want you to think I would keep you in a class if the teacher truly did not like you. She wants you to learn and she wants you to be able to let her teach. So, again, is there something that happened at school today that you need to tell me about?" Lynn Hannigan asks quietly.

"Mom, I—" Slater starts before she cuts him off.

All at once, she abruptly stands from her stool and takes two small steps toward Slater before she leans in to whisper, looking him in the eyes. "I know—you didn't do it." As she turns to go, she twists her neck to look back and finishes by threatening, "And, Slater—I do not want to find out that this *is* you, or you can say good-bye to Halloween."

All Slater can think is *No, not my Halloween Haunt! I've been planning this since last year's epic party! I already know what I'm doing to top it and no one ever thought I'd be able to! Why does Miss Burbank have to ruin everything for me?*

Slater's silence and the look of terror in his eyes gives his mother the perfect carrot to dangle in front of her son for the next month. She would hate to cancel his Haunt Night. It was such delicious fun last year to scare some of the children belonging to the mothers she is not so fond of anymore. She would only half smile to herself when her friends would confide that some of those children had nightmares for weeks. She cannot wait to see the looks of terror on their faces this year from the devilish fun she and Slater have ramped up.

But, in the end, it is up to Slater to behave.

Dear Miss Burbank,

I want you to know I have received your email and I am sorry you have had such a rough start to your school year. Unfortunately, I am not sure there is more I can offer you in the way of support since Slater tells me he had nothing to do with the class shenanigans today. I know Slater wants to have a positive school year and he is hoping you will teach him something useful. We share in this hope and do not expect that there will be any more need for you to concern yourself about Slater. Hank and I are always available if you believe we should instead meet with Principal Daly.

Regards,

Lynn Hannigan, mother of Slater Hannigan

At six o'clock in the evening, Dana Burbank is still seated at her desk inside Room 14 when a message on her computer screen pops up from Lynn Hannigan. Curious about the response to her detailed email home of what the day held, Miss Burbank opens her mailbox. Only two minutes later, she snaps shut her computer lid and dials the number to the one person who will surely be sympathetic.

"Mom, I can't believe it. She's not even listening to anything I am saying. Of course she believes her son, who is never going to admit to doing anything wrong," Dana Burbank spews to her mother.

"Sweetheart, this is not going to be the end of you. I raised you to be stronger than this. There is no way a child can hold this much power over you. We've gone over this. You need to be the adult here, Dana. I don't know how else to say it. Yes, I know he's making your life miserable, but Bill Daly knows what you're up against and he has asked you to do this because he has confidence in your professionalism," Pearl Burbank says with a hearty dose of candor.

"Mother, it is not that I can't handle Slater; I just wanted you to make me feel better," Dana surrenders.

"Oh, well, if that's all you wanted, then let's pretend you don't have to be professional. I suggest you build a chicken coop next to the vegetable garden and then you mesh together some trip wire so that when Slater looks for a good place to hide, and you know he will, he'll be dangling upside down for the weekend. Imagine if no one could find him until Monday when the kinders go to collect the eggs! Now, that would be fun, wouldn't it?" she says, jesting.

"Thanks, Mama, I needed that," Dana Burbank says cheerfully as she hangs up with her mother. A lingering smile crosses her face as she imagines the sight of Slater bobbing around like an upside-down piñata, with his head only two inches above all of the chicken dung.

The next morning after first greeting her students on the line for Room 14, then shuttling them neatly through the door, Miss Burbank begins with a word of caution for how the rest of the year will roll.

"Class, I have never seen such a spirited group of children as what you presented to me yesterday, on the first day of school no less," she says evenly.

A hand shoots into the air as Sibley White thinks to ask a question.

"Not now, honey. Can I have you wait just a minute, please?" Miss Burbank calmly pacifies Sibley as she continues.

"I did not want to talk about this part on the first day, but you need to know about consequences in this classroom. We are learning about what our founding fathers imagined for our country, and the only way we can function is by having laws from the government that protect us from others who seek to take away our rights.

"This class will operate like a new society with laws in place to protect what each of you is entitled to—a free, public education—and I have been appointed to give that to you. I will not allow anyone in here to rob you of this right.

"For those who will try to abuse their own power of citizenship, I have a long, juicy list of debts you will need to repay to your society. These debts will depend on your crimes against our society.

"So, now there is only one question that remains. As you judge those who are robbing you of your rights, you need to determine first the rights you feel entitled to as a society, and the debts you feel should be paid when someone goes against your society's expectations.

"I am separating you into small groups of five so you can create your own Constitution on this chart paper I am providing. You only have twenty minutes to come up with five crimes and five punishments. Each person needs to have ownership over one infraction and one debt paid to society. Brainstorm as many ideas as you want, but after twenty minutes, you need your final five.

"Any questions?" Miss Burbank scans the room to find Sibley White's hand.

"Miss Burbank, are we in trouble from yesterday?" Sibley asks nervously. She has never been in trouble before, and this worry has kept her up all night long.

"Oh, Sibley, certainly *you* are not in trouble." She offers a reassuring smile. "But let's just say yesterday is behind us, and I think by the time we post our Constitution this afternoon, we are going to have a very clear understanding of what this year is going to look like as far as behavior expectations are concerned," Miss Burbank says with a lingering stare toward Slater's row.

While students are sorted into their small groups and desks are awkwardly moved together to form an uneven cluster, Miss Burbank hands each student a different colored marker to record his or her contribution so she will know who is participating in earnest.

"Hey, Slater, what should the punishment be for throwing rubber balls?" Macaroni jests. He and Slater haven't ever been in a class together, and since Macaroni is not very athletic, they don't play together on any sports teams, either. But their mothers are good friends and have made sure to schedule play dates for them ever since the first grade.

"You know what I think? I think there should be no punishment if nobody gets hurt," Slater boasts.

"That's a good one," Macaroni says, nodding his head and drawing a picture of a tank with his green marker.

"I think Miss Burbank wants us to take this seriously," Sibley White chimes in.

"I am being serious. Nobody got hurt, so nobody should pay," Slater says sincerely.

"But, what about us getting robbed of our right to an education? Some of us do want to learn something this year. What is the punishment for someone who tries to waste class time?" Sibley says, holding her ground.

Slater does not care for Sibley White at all. She has always been the kid who has to have an answer for every single question. She gets every award there is and never does anything interesting except read those big books she likes to lug around.

"Yeah, what about making that person serve detention for disrupting the lesson?" Kelly Greenly chimes in to support Sibley White.

"Ooh, I think that person should also have to pick up one piece of litter on campus for every minute the class has to stop learning," Trinity Lee adds enthusiastically.

"Yeah, write that down too," Sibley White says, naturally taking the lead.

As the morning's activity progresses, Miss Burbank observes the jibber jabber from her students about what rights they feel entitled to in the classroom. Some of the debts to be paid to society are worse than anything Miss Burbank would ever think to use as a punishment—and this pleases her immensely.

Every student group includes loud protests over why a law that is only important to *one* person should have to be followed by the whole class, especially if it's not even that big of a deal.

Ask Jody Bryant if getting gum stuck in her hair is a big deal. She believes someone should be punished for the hour she endured of her mother tugging at her scalp with a comb before finally giving up and cutting Jody's hair into a pixie cut that made her look like a boy for most of the fourth grade. There should be a law against gum chewing in class.

By the time this process is fully debated, revised accordingly, and voted on with a class majority, the fifth graders in Room 14 have come up with quite a clever list for their Constitution.

"We believe that our society will function more perfectly if all citizens have the right to:

1—Education without disruption," Sibley White proudly reads from the final class chart.

Tobey picks up where Sibley leaves off. "2—Be heard because every opinion matters, and 3—Our stuff being safe (no stealing, ruining, or using personal possessions without permission)."

"4—Kindness from everyone in Room 14 (no mean comments)," Trinity Lee says.

"5—A safe room (no throwing objects or running), and 6—Quiet time for at least thirty minutes a day," Neimer reads quietly, looking at Miss Burbank, hoping this last one is not too much to ask.

"7—Homework-free weekends, and 8—Homework passes every month, and 9—A study guide before every test, and 10—An award for every student at report card time."

Satisfied that her students have set up the year's expectations in a way that they can police each other, Miss Burbank gets back to teaching. She teaches grammar and science and a love of writing. Her favorite theme to teach comes in the form of scary Halloween poems.

On the morning of October 16th, students walk into a room they hardly recognize. Miss Burbank stayed late the night before to hang cobwebs made of cotton batting strung diagonally from wall to wall. She has set out jack-o-lanterns with menacing expressions reserved for each student, their name tags beneath written in her best spooky scrawl. Her collection of dozens of wing-spanned bats hangs from wires above the desks, where the ones with built-in sensors will screech violently if touched. Best of all, she plays her chilling goblin music as the children cross her learning threshold.

"Moo-ah-ha-ha," laughs the ghost with his sinister deep voice booming from the CD stereo speakers.

"This is so cool," Macaroni says to Tobey and Slater.

"If you like this, you should see what I'm doing for my Halloween Haunt this year," Slater says with a glimmer in his eye.

"Can I come?" both of the boys say eagerly at once.

"Dude, you won't believe it when you see the invitations. They look like they are written in real dried-up blood, like somebody had to scratch their last wishes into a wall with their long fingernails before they died," Slater says eerily, hoping to terrify them just a bit.

"Oh, man, I can hardly wait!" Tobey squeals.

On the same day Miss Burbank teaches *The Raven* by Edgar Allen Poe, with the challenge for each of her students to then create their own scary Halloween poem using the same rhyming meter and number of stanzas, Slater Hannigan passes out invitations for his long-awaited Halloween Haunt.

> *You are cordially invited to Slater Hannigan's*
> *Halloween Haunt if you dare.*

> *Beware, may cause severe nightmares. Do not come if*
> *you are under the age of fifth grade. Meet at Higgins*
> *Mortuary (the old farm next to the closed bowling*
> *alley) before sunset. Best costumes win a grand prize.*

His flyer is hastily distributed up and down the aisles while Miss Burbank grades at her desk with the lights dimmed as the theme music plays. Shrills of excitement are stifled with fake coughs whenever the teacher looks up from her desk. The memory of last year's Hannigan Haunt is still fresh in the minds of those who were lucky enough to attend. Some parents think that fourth grade is still a little young to terrorize children, even if it is all in good fun.

Finally, Halloween arrives on the last Saturday of the month. Even the meteorologists have conspired to create the perfect setting for Slater's party. The whipping winds have been downgraded to soft breezes, and while there will be no rain in sight, the call for sensational thunder and cracks of lightning will make the evening even more sinister indeed.

Slater and his mom have planned every last detail together. They scared Graham out of his wits after turning off all of the living room lights, allowing only the flickering candles to be their backdrop as they practiced talking to each other in cackling voices. Nothing ever frightens Slater. He gets it from his mom, who threw her own Halloween bashes when she was in college. She would decorate the entire dorm and have truth-or-dare sessions that would spook even some of the toughest guys. That's how Slater's parents met. His dad fell for one of her dares and decided that she was more clever than most of the other college co-eds, and they have been having fun ever since.

Graham, though, is still too young for fright night. Lynn says the family can't punish him with their evil wit because it will make him cry. And once Graham starts crying, he cannot stop.

CHAPTER 5

Higgins Mortuary

Higgins Mortuary is a sign that only exists for Slater Hannigan's party. Lynn Hannigan pays $2,700 to rent the farm that Farmer Higgins will turn into a real-life cemetery for one night. Chester Higgins retired the farm but kept the land for event space to be used all year. Every Halloween, he knows the Hannigans will want him to create something even better than the year before.

So for two months now, he has been following Lynn's instructions. Make headstones out of wood then paint them grey so they look real. Lynn asked him to create different shapes of tombstones that would be big enough for a fifth grader to hide behind. The other detail that has taken him some time to create is to make personalized custom epitaphs for every invited guest. The entire farm now looks like a graveyard straight out of some vampire movie. His final charge is to dress the part of the scary gravedigger and explain the haunting rules to guests before the night begins. This is always his favorite part.

To be sure to look his worst, Farmer Higgins avoids shaving for a week. His grey beard grows scraggly and itches him, so he scratches regularly as he talks. He adjusts his voice so everything he says has a bit of a squeak, and he speaks slowly as if he is not sure he should be sharing the fate that lies ahead.

Farmer Higgins knows how to build tension. He used to be in drama when he was in college fifty years earlier. He never went on to do any plays, but he sure did love to spin a good story.

He dresses like you might imagine a scarecrow to look. His dusty brown overalls have been made that way from rolling them in the mud during the last rains. His flannel shirt is untucked from one side, hanging out loosely above the pocket. He wears an oversized tweed sports coat that is rumpled where the sleeves are rolled up to reveal heavy black gardening gloves splattered in dried paint—the same color as blood.

He wears an old chapeau with a leather belt around its brim. It looks weathered, and so does he. Instead of a corncob pipe, he twirls a toothpick in his mouth and holds a shovel as tall as himself. He creates the impression that he's dug a fresh hole for one of these guests here tonight without ever having to say as much. Instead, he begins with his scripted greeting.

"On this Hallowed Eve, there will be horrors for those of you here who've dared to disturb the dead. You've got some nerve showing here tonight, but you don't look that brave to me. If you can stand the howling, you might be ready for the rest of yer challenge.

"Cross the graveyard without yer cryin' or pleadin' and there's sure to be a prize for ya, something fer yer troubles, let's say. But, if you ain't able to see yer way clear to the other side because we hear yer screamin' from some hand that just grabbed yer ankle tryin' to pull ya down into that grave, then be prepared for such an insufferable night of being chased by ghouls through the tunnel maze beneath us, the likes which'll give ya nightmares fer weeks out."

The silent gulps of Tobey, Macaroni, and the other boys can be heard from within the crowd all gathered around in complete and utter silence. The girls look at each other with quivering lips and clutch hands tightly together in bands of three and four because nobody wants to be separated from their group now.

Farmer Higgins continues, "As a bonus to ya, there's braggin' rights to be had if yer able to find yer own grave markings and take a picture of yerself with it. Don't be too surprised if the witch comes out of the fog and mist to describe the kind of death that awaits yer in this lifetime. Consider it our parting gift to yer, a little look into yer crystal ball.

"He, he, he, he, he," he cackles, howls, and coughs all at once. His character acting could have won him an Oscar indeed if he had ever taken more than that one theater class. "Fastest one to make it back to the mortuary wins dinner with the witches next weekend."

Electricity is in the air, and it has nothing to do with the quaking noises of the thunder far off in the distance. Before the scavenger hunt through the cemetery even begins, four kids call home so they can be picked up right now. Sibley White is the first to leave. She at least attempted to make friends by coming here tonight. But everyone knew Sibley would never make it through the entire evening, not if it was anything like last year. And tonight will prove to be nothing at all like last year.

In fact, Slater is already quite pleased with himself. He knows it's all an act, but even he feels a chill running down his spine. Maybe his mom planned a special surprise for him, too? He wouldn't put it past her.

"Get yerselves into yer feeble clusters of five. Only five at a time get to cross the graves of those who've dared to go before yer," Farmer Higgins continues in his crackly voice.

The children all arm themselves by holding onto their dinosaur tails, or the robot control panel pasted onto the silver-painted cardboard box housing them inside. The first group to go forward includes Phil Moore, Tobey Peterson—and Joe Maroney, the one everyone calls Macaroni because he likes a nickname. Some of the girls from class push in to huddle behind some of the toughest boys in class. Besides, who wants to stay behind with Neimer the Weiner anyway?

"Hey, you girls better not distract us. We don't want to go down no graves because you are all screaming and sniveling," Phil says, nervously looking around to make sure he is not stepping near any open trenches.

"I think the fastest way to cross the cemetery is to just go row by row, with everyone together," Laurie Trimball whispers.

"How 'bout you girls go on one side and us guys will go on the other side, and whoever finds our headstones calls out our names," Tobey says in such a brave voice. The kid who can't even swim is feeling quite sure that nothing will go wrong for him tonight. He's not afraid of an underground tunnel.

"I suppose the longer we stand here, the longer it will take us to get across to the other side," Kerry Ko says decidedly.

Together, they agree they will split up to venture across the aisles of markers looking for one another's names, taking care to not get grabbed by the ankles.

Within the first two minutes, Phil yells Laurie's name. The girls all come at once, hands still clasped together, clinging to each other.

"I found yours. It says you die in ten years when you are twenty years old. Quick, pull out your phone and I'll take a picture of you," Phil rattles off commands.

"Is there a witch lurking around here? I want to get out of here before she comes," Laurie says, wrestling with the layers of fabric on her princess skirt to get at the phone she has tucked into her jean pants pocket beneath.

"Aaaargh, what're yer doin' in my yard on this here hallowed night?" cries a ghastly looking witch with green skin and a long, pointed nose. She is all done up to look like any other witch in an all-black tattered dress and pointed hat, but instead of carrying a broomstick, this one has a spear with a crystal ball on the end.

"Ahhhh! you scared me so bad!" Phil screams and punches the air in front of him twice.

The witch continues in her best cackling voice, "Ah, but my dear, the only thing you have to fear is death itself. Let us see how you will be exiting this little party." Just then two hands reach up from the open grave, grabbing at Phil's ankles. He is pulled down into a torch-lit tunnel where, all alone, he will be chased by ghouls—the only ones who know the way out.

"Ahhhhh!" is the only sound Phil makes before his faint screaming disappears into silence.

"Noooo! Please, I want to go home!" Laurie says shakily as she starts to cry. She untangles herself from Kerry's grip and runs as fast as she can across the field, screaming all the way.

"Well, my dear, I see your little friends are not as brave as you," she speaks slowly, stroking the top of the glass ornament. "Would you like to know your fate?"

"Actually, I would," Kerry quickly replies, "and please be fast. I want to win the first-place prize."

Surprised by her lack of power over this little girl's fearlessness, the witch gives the regular rundown. "On a dark and stormy night, much like tonight—"

"But it's not raining tonight, so how could my fate be like tonight if it's not raining?"

"Okay, on a dark and *nearly* stormy night, you will be driving down a deserted highway, cool wind in your hair—"

"Wait, am I in a song? My dad plays that album over and over. Who's that band again?"

"It's the Eagles, and no, you're not in a song. Here's how your life really ends." The witch's cackle begins to sound like an annoyed waitress now as she continues, "You're not in a car. You're running on a pathway with only the moonlight shining above. You hear a noise behind you, and as you turn to look, you don't see the edge of the cliff in front of you, so you fall to your death and drown in the ocean waves below."

"That works for me. Can you please stand here while we take a picture now?" Kerry Ko turns to Tobey, handing him her phone. "Tobey, take the photo, let's get moving."

Click. Kerry says sayonara to the group and runs ahead to cross that finish line first.

Left alone after the witch creeps behind another tombstone, Tobey and Macaroni look at each other. "Um, let's get outta here," Macaroni says nervously.

"We will just as soon as we find my grave. I'm not letting Kerry Ko be the only one to cross to the other side," Tobey whispers, angling which aisle to pursue.

"I'm staying for like two minutes and then I'm gone. This place creeps me out," Macaroni says, his ferocious gorilla mitt hand holding his tiny statue of the Empire State Building.

A noise that sounds like twigs snapping two rows over leaves both boys frozen. They stand perfectly motionless, trying to see what they can make out through the fog. The dry ice everywhere is doing its job to create the most convincing atmosphere to scare impressionable children.

"Did that come from over there? Do you think it's another witch coming to get us?" Macaroni asks in a panic.

"Mac, be quiet, I can't—" Tobey is cut off midstream when he is grabbed by the cuffs of his Peter Pan booties, pulled down through the grave into the caverns below.

"Aaaaaahhh!" Macaroni also lets out a long wail as he falls at the same time Tobey slides beside him. The two of them in the ridiculous costumes their stage mothers sewed at home hold hands tightly, clinging to the hopes that someone will hear their screams.

All at once, the graveyard is drenched in darkness. All of the torches go out, but a rattling noise echoes from up ahead.

"Oh, man, I want to get outta here," Macaroni says slowly and softly, hoping to not let the boogeyman hear him.

"They're trying to scare us. It's all fake, though; Slater planned it this way," Tobey says with a false confidence as his voice quivers.

Ching, ching, ching, clang, clang. The chains sound heavy as they drag along the floor of the corridor up ahead.

"Umm, I am not g-g-going down there. L-l-let's just wait here until-l-l someone el-else drops through the grave," Macaroni says, trembling so much his words shake.

"Man, we've got to run for it. They're trying to freak us out. They'll never expect us to run toward the chains. Let's just go, come on," Tobey says convincingly. Who would have ever thought the kid who couldn't swim at the water park last year would be this brave in a dark tunnel?

"Dude, I—" Macaroni is hoisted away from his safe spot when Tobey grabs his arm so hard Macaroni has no choice but to keep running. "Ruunn, ruunn, there's no way out for youuuuu!" blares a low bellow that echoes through the crude cave-like walls.

"Let's go! Come on, this way," Tobey barks orders to Macaroni. Tobey keeps sliding around corners in his soft, felt Peter Pan slippers while Macaroni throws his gorilla mitts and hair hat behind him as clues that they were here—in case they are never found alive again. "Muwaaaa-aah-aaah-hah!" sneers the evil laughter from behind them.

Then, just there in front of them, a ghoul appears in tattered rags with a torch made to glow like a fire stick, but it is really just orange cellophane paper over a flashlight.

"Who dares to enter my halls? Gone, be gone with you!" he angrily shouts as he blocks the one entrance the boys were sure to have taken. The mistake is an unfortunate one because that entrance leads to a corner meant to hold firewood logs for the mortuary's fireplace upstairs. Just a dead end, that's all—unless someone were to lean against the fake bundle of wood, discovering a hidden stairwell behind it leading upstairs to the mortuary's own kitchen. Nope, no shortcuts for Tobey and Macaroni.

With a few more zigzags like this, the boys are utterly petrified. They are chased around corners darkened and misted over with more dry ice until they are finally, and thankfully, reunited with

Phil, who is already finishing his warm apple pie and cold milk. The end of the chamber is the last gathering place for all who have finished the graveyard jaunt.

"Dudes, you made it! Took you long enough! I've been waiting here for like twenty minutes!" Phil says excitedly with his mouth still full of pie crust.

"Awww, man, we thought you were a goner for sure," Macaroni says with a smile.

"For sure!" Tobey agrees heartily. "You were screaming so bad, you sounded like my little sister when I cut her Barbie's hair off," he says, rolling backward laughing.

The boys begin to relax and reel off their adventure of how they managed to get away from every monster in the caverns no matter how fast they were being chased. The exaggerations grow with each retelling, and by the time the whole class reunites, Slater is backslapped and punched in the arm while all of his friends tell him what a sonic party this was.

Every group has had their turn at crossing the cemetery, and every group has similar stories to tell. Of course, Kerry Ko is the only one brave enough to annoy her witch for the weak plot points she was initially given, but even Kerry had a good time watching everyone else cross the finish line behind her.

What half of the class never got to hear was the witch's prediction for Slater's own fate. This is the real ghost story now being shared in whispers, adding a chill to the foggy night air. While his classmates beg for a full repeat, even Slater has to look around to make sure his is not the only face turning pale at the prospect of hearing it again.

CHAPTER 6

Slater's Fate

"Hey, get a load of Slater. He doesn't look so good," Tobey whispers to Macaroni.

"He's probably just wishin' he could've gotten dragged through the tunnels too. You know how he loves that stuff," Macaroni whispers back.

"I, for one, would love to know what Slater's fate held from that witch who tried to tell me that I was doomed on a dark and stormy night much like tonight. As if," Kerry Ko says to provoke someone into finally telling what the mysterious future holds for Slater.

While a few kids still graze from the boxes holding the last of the pizza slices now cooled from the night air, most already sit on bundles of twine-tied haystacks big enough to accommodate the bottoms of four friends. They eat the desserts they have greedily pulled from the towering tiers of cupcakes made to look like a green goblin, with each one fitted into the puzzle of a monster's face—disfigured, with a haunting expression of a ghoul screaming. The top tier is decorated in toasted coconut painted with silver food spray to look like hair. The tier beneath is made to look like the skin that has come from a sea creature, with slime of green seaweed made believable from edible leaves trailing down the sides of the wrapper.

In the center of the face are the blackest paper wrappers to build the gigantic pupils laced in licorice slivers to give the impression of lashes made to look like spiders coming out of its eyes.

The cupcakes full of cherry pie toppings represent the monster's bloody mouth—the same red jelly that is now dripping from the children's chins. Their little fingers clench more tightly as they slowly strangle their second helping—unaware of the jelly mess within their grips—while they listen intently to the story of Slater's fate unfolding.

"Fer those of you who were nowhere to be found when yer little friend here was given the crystal ball readin' for the rest of his short life, we'll give it to ya again, that is if it's not too much for yer to handle." Farmer Higgins stirs the crowd.

"I'm not afraid. It's just a story anyway," Slater rebuffs. But something has him shaken. It's not what he says, but how he says it. Slater is always the kid to go first on any dare. What has him spooked about this witch's tale is about to be discovered by all of his friends.

"Hagitha, will yer be able to use yer seeing powers to share this young man's fate one more time with the crowd?" Farmer Higgins says, pointing his shovel dramatically toward Slater.

"Oh, dearie," she replies in a cackling call from behind the crowd, appearing from just a vapor of dry ice, "it would be my pleasure." Already, the girls sitting on haystacks move in tighter toward one another.

"It appears that you will be leaving this world the same way that you came in, kicking and screaming, afraid of what is about to grab you," Hagitha says slowly.

Her hands twist around her crystal ball as if to move the fog out of the way, pretending to see more clearly the real images inside.

"Sadly, your gravestone has markings that look like you do not go to your death easily. There is claw scratching all across the front where your name is engraved, and only the first three digits of the last year of your life remain. 202—."

"Get to the part where Slater dies," Kerry Ko says, hoping to bait this witch into coming up with a more original storyline than the one she got.

"Good things come to those who wait, my pretty," Hagitha says without looking up from her sphere.

Kerry Ko rolls her eyes while she strokes her long, jet-black hair of silk—a habit that calms her nerves.

"In the dark of the night, on a plateau where wild animals will not even dare to roam, you will find yourself alone, without friends, clinging to life. Your fingernails will claw the earth to keep you from falling to your death." She pauses to extend her pointy finger toward Slater's chest.

"Nobody is coming to your rescue. Nobody can hear your cries," she hisses, looking up from her ball. "Nobody knows where you have gone.

"Unless you can save yourself before dawn, the crows will be waiting to peck out your eyes at sun's first light." Hagitha ends her words with a long drawl and tilts her head to shift her gaze directly upon Slater. "Such a pitiful way to go, my precious. You have such pretty eyes, too."

It is absolutely silent. A perfect slice of moon shines above the outdoor gathering. The air has turned chilly and the kids finally realize that they have been sitting motionless with mouths full of pizza that have not yet been chewed.

"Yeah, that's a pretty good story, witch," Slater reels off coolly, nervously tossing glances toward his classmates, wondering if they buy any of this. He knows it's not like anyone can really predict the future. There is no such thing as magic.

"Off to the devil with you then, my child," Hagitha says as she tips her pointed hat and snaps her fingers, disappearing through a trap door beneath her poof of mist.

"Slater, this was such a cool party. You should have seen Molly Weinstein. I think she is still chewing on her braids," Kerry Ko says to Slater as if to congratulate him on the sport of entertainment he created here tonight.

"Hey, Kerry, thanks. I guess you get to have dinner with the witches next week," Slater tosses back. "Nobody even came close to your time."

"Yeah, well, your witch story was better than my witch story, so I was ready to get a move on," Kerry chortled.

Ka-boom! Pow, pow! Bang! Out of nowhere, the kids react to the startling noises that jolt everyone out of their seats—fireworks signaling the party is over.

The sweeping tails of dragon costumes and long princess skirts swish in a flurry as friends jostle to find their waiting cars.

"Mom, Mom, you won't believe how I die," Macaroni says to his mother, who looks up to see where Lynn Hannigan could possibly be hiding.

"Dear, I am sure you are going to live a long and healthy life," she offers reassuringly, knowing full well she will be up with her little Macaroni several times tonight to calm the nightmares he is sure to have.

"Thanks, Slater. Thank you, Mrs. Hannigan," Kerry Ko says politely before she picks up her goody bag full of fortune cookies, tarot cards, and a perfect miniature replica of a crystal ball.

"Seems like your friends had a nice time tonight, honey," Mrs. Hannigan says confidently.

"Mom, it was great! The part when you grabbed their ankles to pull them down the raft slides was awesome. We could hear them screaming for a long time," Slater rattles off excitedly.

"Farmer Higgins and I had a lot of fun beneath those graves," she says with a giggle.

"Hey, that witch was kind of creepy," Slater offers. His mom cannot tell if this is a compliment or if his own prediction has him worried.

"Did you like her story?"

"Yeah, she was cool, but she was kind of creepy, too, like she could really see something in that glass ball of hers," Slater says, trying to be nonchalant.

"Oh, Slater, isn't this half the fun? You love being scared out of your mind, so I answered a few of her questions about how you were born with a set of lungs on you that would not quit and how you used to be afraid of some of those scenes in *Lion King* when you were little, and she just took the rest from there."

"Yeah, it was a pretty good party. Thanks, Mom. I wish Dad could have been here. He would have been an awesome ogre."

"You know how much he wanted to be here, but he's got an important job now and we all said we would understand when he would need to miss family events to help the city stay safe," Lynn says, adding a shrug.

"I know," Slater says as he waves at everyone waving back from behind their parents' car windows.

"Let's go say good-bye to Farmer Higgins, and you be sure to thank him for the bad dreams he will probably be the cause of tonight!" She tussles his hair that still will not move under the lacquered spray of jet-black paint completing his Dracula look.

At school on Monday, a renewed energy is in the air. The students cannot stop talking about Slater's Halloween Haunt, and Miss Burbank overhears all of their excitement.

"Let's get back to work, children," she says from her desk.

"Excuse me, Miss Burbank. We're from student council, and we were wondering if we could make an announcement?" Gina Gomez and Charity Bronstein are both fifth graders from Mr. McCloud's class. Neither of them would ever have been comfortable enough to walk into a classroom of students they did not know until they had Miss Burbank as a teacher last year. They remain some of her favorite students.

"Hi, girls. Sure, come on in if it will take you only a couple of minutes," Miss Burbank says with a warm hug for each of them. "Class, we have an important announcement from student council, so please pay close attention for just a moment to Gina and Charity, who have something to share."

"Hi, guys. I'm Gina."

"And I'm Charity."

"And we just wanted to tell you about a school fund-raiser we are holding before Thanksgiving break," Gina begins with real enthusiasm. "It's called the Thanksgiving Pie Challenge."

"Every single class on campus will have a contest to raise the most money donated by students. This money goes toward buying the yearbooks so everyone can get a discount price," Charity continues and is about to discuss the exciting part when Gina chimes in.

"If you collect $100 from your class, you will get to pie your teacher in the face with a whipped cream pie, and then for being such a good sport, your teacher will get to take a real pumpkin pie home for the holidays," Gina says, enthusiastically waving her hands when she imitates smashing a pie into a teacher's face.

"This by no means is a disrespect to our teachers, so any teacher who does not want to be pied in the face can pay a fine to skip the challenge if their class raises enough money. It's only $10 to get out of being pied," Charity says, turning her head to face Miss Burbank.

"It's for a really good cause since we all want our fifth-grade yearbooks for graduation, and the printing costs keep going up every year," Gina offers persuasively.

"So, do you guys have any questions?"

Lots of hands shoot in the air. Most of them come from the back corner of the room.

"Hi, Macaroni, what's your question?"

"Well, what if we raise more than the hundred bucks needed to pie a teacher? What do we kids get? Do we get our own pie if one of us raises the most money?" Macaroni is obviously thinking about how he can get his own pumpkin pie.

"If one of you raises a lot more money than anyone else in class, it will be up to your teacher if you get something special. Some teachers are going to give *their* pie to the kid who donates the most money, while other teachers are thinking of allowing a student to take the pie in the face if the teacher pays the forfeit fee," Charity explains.

"Slater, what's your question?"

"Let's say we raise $300 as a class; can we get *three* pies for the top three donators?"

"Um, we don't know about that because—well—" Gina begins before she is cut off entirely from Charity, who seems to be making up rules to look like she knows it all.

"Slater, if your class brings in $300, then we will see about getting you two more pies," Charity says matter-of-factly. The power surge going straight to her head makes her feel so important, she forgets she has no real authority over promising anything.

"Okay, girls, thank you for the information about the Thanksgiving Pie Challenge. I'm sure our class will be very excited to see what we can do about raising funds to support yearbook discounts for everyone," Miss Burbank says, squinting at the flyer.

✐   ✐   ✐   ✐

During lunch inside the teacher's lounge today, the faculty members are sharing stories of their weekends at home, grading or watching football or planting gardens until talk turns to who is willingly participating in the Thanksgiving Pie Challenge.

"I will happily be paying the ten dollars required to forfeit. There is no way I am walking around with whipped cream in my hair for the rest of the day," Miss Cherie Carlson, one of the fourth grade teachers, says affirmatively.

"Oh, I think it's a cute idea. I doubt my class will be able to raise that much money, so I don't have to worry," Rita Jensen, a second-grade teacher, chimes in.

"I don't know. I get a sense that Slater and some of his friends would like to raise enough to get three pies," Miss Burbank says, sounding worried.

"If he brings in the whole hundred dollars, Dana, are you going to go along and let him pie you in the face?" Rita says aloud, getting everyone else to wave their forks around as they all weigh in on what this could look like.

"Oh, I do not even want to think about it. If Slater gets his hands on a hundred dollars, I will come up with some other way for him to get his fun. There is no way that child is going to pie me in the face," Dana says assuredly, wiping ranch dressing from the corners of her mouth.

All of the other teachers nod in agreement and can't wait to see how much money Room 14 will be raising. In the three weeks left to go before the Thanksgiving Pie Challenge, other matters will become more pressing.

The next morning at school, the students find a brown paper bag taped to the wall outside of Room 14. A note is written upon it in red paint with squiggly brush lines of crooked lettering and paint drippings dried in sloppy puddles at the bottom of each character. On the front of the large grocery sack, in a font resembling claw marks—stretching each letter to look longer than normal—the words from Slater's fate are printed:

In the dark of the night, on a plateau where wild animals will not even dare to roam, you will find yourself alone, without friends, clinging to life. Your fingernails will claw the earth to keep you from falling to your death. Nobody is coming to your rescue. Nobody can hear your cries. Nobody knows where you have gone.

Unless you can save yourself before dawn, the crows will be waiting to peck out your eyes at sun's first light; such a pitiful way to go, my precious. You have such pretty eyes, too.

Before the school bell even rings, signaling all children to line up on their classroom number painted on the blacktop, kids from every class hover beneath the bag posting Slater's fateful reading.

The older boys who belong in Room 14 clamor around the crowd and push their way to the front to see what is holding the attention of the fourth and third graders who can read. "Hey, it's Slater's fate," Macaroni says to Tobey.

"How'd that get here?" Tobey wonders aloud.

"What are you guys gawking at?" Slater asks as he moves in to see what has his friends so interested.

When Tobey, Macaroni, and the other guys see Slater, the crowd parts. The younger kids stand frozen as if a legend is walking by, a *living* legend—for now.

"What? How's this? Who did this?" Slater asks, hardly having a chance to process what he sees. Why would someone write out his fate in scary looking letters?—the same kind of scary looking letters he used to make the scary looking invitations for his Halloween Haunt.

Slater jumps for the bag hanging above Room 14 to grab its bottom corner with his fingertips. He is able to tug the paper hard enough on his first try to pull the whole thing down, leaving only bits of masking tape on the painted brick walls.

"I don't know why this is here," Macaroni says, perplexed.

"It's not like it means anything or anything; it was just a stupid story," Slater retorts. "It's not like I even care because my mom paid that lady to be spooky, so it's not even really real," Slater spouts off.

"Sure, no, you're right," Macaroni says wholeheartedly even though his brows are furrowed and his voice sounds less committed than his words.

"Hey, we know it doesn't mean anything, totally just a joke. But who did this and why? That's what we need to find out," Tobey says excitedly, like they have a new mission.

"Am I supposed to be scared? Like is someone thinking I'm supposed to be scared by this stupid thing?" Slater snorts. "Because that is the biggest joke of all. My mom paid, like, a lot of money for that witch to do her acting thing, so it's, like, totally made up." Slater continues to scoff.

"Everybody had a blast at that party, Slater. Nobody who was there would have done this," Phil says confidently.

"But, then," Slater begins slowly, looking at the letters on this bag and quickly scratching under his armpits, "why would someone take the time to write it all down? What's the point?"

The point is that Slater has an enemy. The most popular kid in Miss Burbank's fifth grade who just threw the most epic Halloween Haunt—where everyone had the most epic time getting scared out of their minds and eating awesome pizza and cupcakes—has an enemy. People got big prizes for best costumes and they got pictures with witches and they got to hear spooky stories and meet Farmer Higgins. How could he possibly have an enemy?

Unless, it's just possible, that someone is jealous of Slater Hannigan. That makes more sense to him than anything else because Slater knows how to take care of his friends. But who could have it out for Slater? This is what becomes the true haunting of Slater Hannigan for weeks to come.

CHAPTER 7

Your Father Is Home

"Hey, sporto, how are you this morning?" Hank Hannigan ruffles the pile of hair sticking sideways on top of Graham's bobbing head.

"Hi, Dad," Graham says sleepily, crawling into his father's lap without a worry about the coffee cup now teetering on the island counter after being skimmed by his backside.

"How'd you sleep, kiddo?"

"I had a dream you got us a puppy and it was licking my face when I woke myself up," Graham says, looking straight into his father's eyes, readjusting his reading glasses so they appear lopsided on Hank's face.

"Well, that sounds like a pretty good dream, bud. I wish we had a dog, too, but you know what Mom says," Hank says in a conspiratorial whisper.

"Until we can all take care of ourselves, there will be no more man nor beast entering this house, Graham snickers, imitating his mother by putting both hands firmly on his hips.

"But, Dad, a puppy is not really a beast. A puppy is fluffy and sweet, and I bet Mom would love him. Let's surprise her with one," Graham says excitedly, as if this is the first time he has ever made this suggestion. "She couldn't say no if she woke up and was being licked by a small white fluffy puppy. Right, Dad?"

"Oh, buddy, your mom might say no within about five minutes, and then you and I would both have to live in the doghouse for the rest of the week."

"Could we, Dad? Could we build a doghouse and you and I live in it? That'd be so fun. Let's build a doghouse and we won't let anybody else in, especially Mom," Graham says, all the while giggling as his dad tickles his ribs until he throws his head back, nearly conking his skull on the marble countertop.

"Why don't you run upstairs and go pounce on your brother like you're a little puppy and wake him up by licking his face? It's time to get the day started for our park adventure."

"Yippee! Hey Slater, wake up, today's the day we're all going to the woods," Graham calls boisterously up the stairs, padding his way to the top of the steps like a little dog climbing on all fours.

"Get out!" Slater says through a pillow that muffles the bellow he intended to be much louder.

"Pounce! I'm a puppy! Wake up, Slater," Graham continues coaxing Slater by jumping on his legs still tucked beneath the twisted covers.

"I'm gonna pounce on *you*, Graham. I was so comfortable. Why'd you have to bug me?"

"Dad says you need to get up. We're going to the forest today. Get up, Slater, it's time to go." Graham keeps taunting Slater by poking him through the covers with his bony heels and trying to stick his toes in Slater's face hiding beneath his flat pillow.

Suddenly, Slater comes from beneath the covers to wrestle Graham in one fell swoop by throwing the blanket over Graham's head to fold his body inside until Graham is hidden away in Slater's burrito roll. Only Graham's feet are dangling outside, wriggling to extricate himself of his brother's stealth move that only superheroes use on their enemies in the movies.

"Arrgghh, Slater, let me out, I can't breathe in here!" Graham wildly protests.

"Oh, I'm gonna let you out as soon as I let something else out. Ready, set, open your mouth to get a good whiff of this," Slater says, torturing his little brother with the odor from the enchiladas and beans Slater had for dinner last night.

As the bubbles come out in a rapid succession, sounding more like snapping plastic from packing wrap, even Mom can hear Graham's protests from downstairs.

"Ewwww, Slater, you stink. Let me outta here. I can't breathe."

Just then, Lynn sprints up the stairs two at a time, darting toward Slater and throwing the covers back so Graham can finally get to freedom. "Slater, get up. Your father's downstairs, and today you are all going to the woods. You've got a fun day ahead, and I expect you to look out for your brother and to not be torturing him." She smooths out the wrinkles of the top covers.

"Mom, why does Graham have to come? He's too young and so are all of his friends. It should just be me and my friends and our dads only," Slater says, trying to poke Graham by extending his leg from his bed.

"Do you know, on second thought, I think this bed needs to be pulled apart because it's time for you to change these sheets. March downstairs and start this blanket in the laundry, and then by the time you have your bed made, breakfast will be ready. Hut, two," she says definitively. "If you want something to complain about, I will give you something to complain about. There are two more beds waiting to be changed today that I could use a little help with if you'd like to stay home and let Graham join his friends and their fathers without you."

"No, I'm going," Slater says loudly before muttering under his breath, "I just don't want Graham to come." He looks directly at Graham with a glint in his eye—always the telltale sign to Graham that he is about to be thrown to the carpet again before Slater will sit on his face to execute some more bubbles.

"Aaargh, Mom, Slater's jumping on me again," Graham screams wildly just in the nick of time.

"Graham, come down here and help me with breakfast while Slater does his chores."

"Ha, ha, you didn't get me," Graham says, wiggling his hips back and forth in a rhythm while he sings his little neener-neener song.

"Oh, just wait, Graham. When you least expect it, expect it," Slater says, tossing a pillow erratically toward Graham's head. Fortunately, Graham knows when to make a run for it, so his little feet are already half sliding down the staircase as he skips three at a time holding clumsily to the banister that keeps him from spilling his marbles down the rest of the steps.

"I'm here, Mom," Graham says. He sniffs over the chocolate chip pancakes, hoping that one will magically jump from the platter into his nose if he inhales deeply enough.

"Graham, go set the table please and then start carrying in these glasses," Lynn directs.

"A fork for Dad, a fork for Mom, a fork for stupid Slater, and a fork for handsome me," Graham says aloud to no one in particular while he walks around the table in duck, duck, goose fashion. "A spoon for Dad, a spoon for Mom, a spoon for stinky Slater, and a spoon for lucky me."

"What is he doing out there talking to himself?" Hank asks his wife with a grin on his face after he peeks through the swinging kitchen door.

"He's setting the table and we're about to eat. Where is that Slater?" Lynn asks. She carries four bowls of sliced strawberries, a smaller dish of whipped cream, and three bananas for her family since she already ate hers while she was flipping pancakes. "Slaaaaater, I'm counting to three, and those beds better be made and you better be down here for breakfast! One, two—" Lynn says as she is cut short by the ghost coming down the staircase.

Wearing all of the dirty bed sheets and blankets over his head after changing the linens from the other two bedrooms, Slater pretends to be a mummy with his arms outstretched in front of him. Without a worry for what could happen if he misses a step or gets his foot caught up in the blankets draping around his ankles, Slater squeals, "Moooo-ah-ah-ah! Graaaa-hammmmm, I'm coming to get you." He descends the staircase, clomping one heavy slipper onto each step.

"Mom, make him stop it," Graham says, picking up his fork and holding it out in front of him in case he needs to defend himself.

"Slater, come sit down and drop that laundry in the garage like your mother asked you to," Hank chimes in without looking up from his newspaper.

"Aw, you guys are no fun," Slater says, pulling the layers of bedding off of his head, leaving him with hair that stands straight up.

"Hey, I want to have static hair, too. Rub those blankets on my head." Graham gallops over to Slater.

"I'm going to give you static hair." Slater swirls the blankets around Graham, tucking him in like a burrito roll all over again, until finally Lynn has had enough.

"Boys, your pancakes are getting cold and your father is waiting. Let's eat so you can go meet your friends," she says exasperatedly.

Both boys chow down pancakes topped with strawberries, banana, and whipped cream. They gulp from their superhero cups and wipe their milk moustaches with the back of their pajama sleeves, forgetting to use the napkins Graham put out. Lynn looks at her husband, who is completely engrossed in the politics section of the paper and smiles to herself. These two wild babies have grown into two wild young hooligans with syrup smears all over their faces and hair standing up as if they have been electrocuted. It is not the family she dreamed of—it's even better.

"Okay, everybody, time to get your hair combed, teeth brushed, clothes on, and not over your pajamas this time."

"I am going to beat you to the car, and then I'm sitting in front," Graham challenges Slater.

"Uh, I'm the oldest, so I sit in front. Doesn't even matter if you beat me, which you won't," Slater shoots back, hightailing it up the staircase, throwing Graham to the wall opposite the banister just vigorously enough to prevent him from getting ahead.

In the bathroom, both boys rush to comb their hair at their dual sinks and mirrors. Slater pulls his old trick of fake brushing by just putting some toothpaste on his tongue and rinsing his mouth. He charges into his room and puts on his jeans, the Beastie Boys concert shirt his dad saved from when he was in high school, and his hoodie. He moves so fast and thunders downstairs so quickly that when he pops open the front door to see Graham already in the front seat of the minivan, he cannot believe his eyes.

"Hey, how'd *you* get out here so fast?"

"Changed in the car," Graham says, smiling ear to ear with that toothless grin.

"Dad, tell Graham to move. It's not fair; I'm older." Slater reels off every point he can think to negotiate for what he wants.

"Slater, did you brush your teeth?"

"Smell my breath."

"I can smell your breath from here. Let me ask you a direct question, did you brush your teeth or just swirl some toothpaste in your mouth?" Dad asks with a full-on gaze straight into Slater's eyes.

"Dad," Slater whines.

"Slater, we can leave whenever you're ready. It does not matter to me if we are the last ones to arrive or if they've already fired up hot dogs and put away lunch by the time we show up; choice is yours."

Slater gets out of the car in a huff, wishing he were in the front seat so he could at least have the satisfaction of slamming the car door—instead of fighting against the minivan slider that glides at the pace of a snail. He sneers at Graham as he walks by the rolled-up car window. From behind its protective glass, Graham sticks out his tongue, showing off his fresh teeth by pulling his cheeks apart with his little fingers.

During the ride to the state park, Dad tries to engage the boys in conversation and take Slater's mind off of the indignity he is suffering by being relegated to sitting in the backseat.

"So, you want to know what case I'm working on now?"

"Oooh, yeah, Dad, tell us. Is it another investigation with a bank robber this time?" Graham asks wide-eyed.

The last story Hank shared with his boys was about a man named Ted "the Lead" Devine. He earned his nickname because he liked to steal cars and run them real fast along the freeways, making the cops chase him really fast, getting "the lead out." He thought he was a daredevil but he was not as good a driver as those guys in Hollywood movies. Even though he was able to outrun and hide from the police in four different car chases after stealing four different cars, he had a ton of close calls where he nearly ran into walls and light poles. Finally, his fifth car ended up running out of gas and he got caught in the middle of the chase. It's *how* their Dad tells the story that keeps them wanting more.

"As a matter of fact, Graham, this one does involve a bank robber by the name of Zero. We don't know his real name yet, but we are getting close. He thinks he has zero chance of getting caught, but—" Hank gets interrupted by his beaming son.

"But, you catch all the bad guys, don't you, Dad?" Graham says, smiling.

"Slater, you want to know what the best part of this investigation is?" Hank asks, eyeing his older son in the rearview mirror.

"No," Slater says, still sulking.

"I get to be home for dinners the next few weeks because Zero only robs banks in the morning," Hank says with a small smile.

"Goody, we can watch some movies after dinner and you can read me my stories," Graham says excitedly.

"-Kay," Slater says, looking out the window. "How soon before we get there?"

"Just a couple more exits up ahead. We're turning off at Willow Glenn, Route 232," Dad says, letting out a slow whistle. "Looks like we're going to need some gas ourselves before we even get there," he says, eyeing the needle reading empty on his tank gauge.

"Boys, you need to use the restrooms? I'm pulling over at this next exit."

"I'm good, Dad. What about youuuu, waaay back there in the baaaack?" Graham says to Slater, cupping his hands around his mouth to pretend he is shouting into a canyon that echoes.

"Graham, I'm gonna get you. When you least expect it, expect it," Slater says with his steely stare as if he is trying to mind warp Graham.

Dad returns to the minivan after gassing up, paying the cashier inside, and grabbing a couple of candy bars for the rest of the ride to Willow Glenn Park just a few miles ahead.

"Boys, you know the drill for today, right?"

"Yeah, Dad, we make sure we have our buddy and then we can only go into Martian's Landing or Two Tall Trees Mountain. All other parts of the park are off limits," Graham says, rattling off the rules he has heard a hundred times.

"Slater, what about you?"

"What about me?"

"Son, I'm counting on you to keep an eye out for your brother and to change up this attitude—deal?"

"Deal," Slater says resignedly, knowing he will suffer more if he doesn't cooperate. "But I'm not going to be Graham's buddy. He's got his own friends, and I want to hang out with Macaroni and Phil." Slater protests half-heartedly, hoping to not get punished by having to hang with the adults.

"Don't worry, you will be able to enjoy the day with your friends.

Be sure to say hello to the other dads before you guys go your separate ways," Hank suggests politely.

As Hank searches for a spot to park the minivan, the boys scour the wide open field called Big Willow for any of their friends who might already be playing Frisbee or tag without them. Nobody they know is there.

They do not recognize any of the families barbecuing beneath the open-area grills protected by an overhang in case of rain. They scan the area known as Wild Clover with outdoor picnic tables and barbecue pits beyond Big Willow where they see about twenty kids dashing around or manning the hot dog skewers over the fires that have just begun to blaze.

"Hey, Slater, we're over here," Macaroni shouts, waving both of his arms wildly, signaling that the fun has not yet begun. He is still so far away from the action that Macaroni's words sound like a muffled roar.

"We're coming," Slater calls back, cupping his hands around his mouth so his voice can carry across the field.

"Dad, can I run over there?" Slater asks eagerly.

"Bud, I need you to help carry the ice chest with Graham. It's pretty heavy now that we've loaded it. Just a few more minutes and you guys can be on your way."

As the Hannigan family lugs their load across Big Willow field, dodging the strangers playing tag and ducking oncoming Frisbees, Slater and Graham renew their feud.

"Hey, Graham, try holding up your end of the chest; you're dragging it," Slater says, annoyed.

"You're going too fast; slow down. I can't hold it because you are going too fast," Graham complains.

All of a sudden the ice chest twists out of Slater's grasp, spilling open the lid and flooding the grass with ice and bottles of water, juice boxes, and soda pop for the kids, whose moms will never know.

"Guys, it's okay. Just shove it all back inside. Doesn't matter if there's grass on the ice; we're not eating the ice," Hank says as he helps the boys push the contents back inside the feeble Igloo their family has had since the kids were toddlers.

"Glad you guys showed." Brent Thompson greets Hank, ruffling the heads of both Hannigan boys. "Good to see you, man."

"Hey, Brent, how you doing? Carol let you out of the house for good behavior?" Hank says, ribbing his old buddy.

"New house, man, never stops. I feel like I'm putting in forty hours on the weekends trying to get that thing painted, get the sod put in, and the deck rebuilt," Brent says as he wipes the sweat off his brows. "Hey, you got anything in that cooler to drink?"

"Yeah, if you don't mind that it's been rolling around in grass." Hank reaches for one of the bottles. "We dropped it and everything went spilling out, but it's still cold."

"Hey, Pete, man, how's it going? I have not seen you since months ago on Father's Day. What is keeping you locked up?" Hank asks his friend who just began flying international trips now that he has gained some seniority with the airlines.

"Buddy, you don't even know the half of it. I have no idea what time zone I'm in right now, but there are some gorgeous parts of the world I am seeing with a front-row view," Pete Driscoll says, bear hugging his friend.

"Good to see you guys. We just don't do this enough," Hank says, slapping his pals on the back. "Let's round up the kids, give them the speech, and then turn them loose," Hank says quickly.

"Boys, huddle—hustle, hustle, let's go," Hank says, clapping his big beefy hands together several times to signal this is lunch.

After the group consumes fifty hot dogs, eight pounds of potato salad, ten big bags of chips, and dozens of drinks, the only food left is the dessert: marshmallows to roast for s'mores. Each of the boys has a stick from the woods that his dad has helped him to shave down into a spear, or a metal hanger brought from home that the dads have unraveled to create a flimsy hook at the end for holding puffy marshmallows.

While the boys slowly chew on heaping mounds of double-stacked layers of chocolate bars and graham crackers with scalding marshmallow oozing from their mouths, this is the perfect time to give reminder instructions of park boundaries and time expectations for checking in with adults.

"Guys, you know the drill, but let's just go over a few safety precautions. Everyone has a buddy, right? We want to see you standing next to your buddy right now," Hank begins seriously. "Good. Now that you are in pairs, or a few of you in trios, we want you to stay in Martian's Landing or Two Tall Trees Mountain only.

Don't roam around any other areas that we have not explored. Also, you need to check in with us face-to-face every two hours. Both of you need to show up; don't just send one buddy. Never separate from your buddy. Got that?" Hank continues with a firm clarity in his voice that holds the attention of all the kids.

"Finally, bring a water for each of you, and tie your coats around your waists. Some of these shaded parts are pretty cool even without our usual November snow. You're hot here in the sun, but you won't be if you're in Martian's Landing. Last thing, don't litter. So whatever you take with you comes back. Are we good?"

Hank Hannigan looks at Slater and Graham, then to his buddies who also eye their sons, and they all seem to be in accordance that he has said what needs to be said. This, after all, is not their first time carting their boys to Willow Glenn for the day. The dads love this trip, maybe even a little more than the kids.

"Okay, guys," Pete Driscoll says enthusiastically, "go have some fun today. See you in two hours."

Even though the boys understand the rules, nobody hears a thing Pete Driscoll says after "go have some fun." Fortunately, they all have watches and know how to tell time. They know how long it takes to get to Martian's Landing and how long it also takes to get to the other side of Two Tall Trees Mountain. They have done this every year for the past four years. This forest is their home. All the nooks and crannies are places they play war games and pretend to shoot the soldier enemies. They know just where to stand on the log that crosses the brook if you want to pee into the stream without falling off on account of the winding moss that is too slippery. They know which kids hang out in which coves, and they know the best sunken-out tree trunks where they can curl up while everyone else calls out their name in a long game of hide-and-seek.

Unfortunately, some of these boys have thought up other plans for new adventures they will have in the forest today.

CHAPTER 8

Olly Olly Oxen Free

"You guys, head over there to Martian's Landing," Slater commands.

"That's not fair. You can't call Martian's Landing just because you're bigger," Graham says in a furtive protest. He knows Slater is still planning some kind of revenge for having to ride in the backseat. "We should ro-sham-bo for it," Graham says decisively while his little friends all nod nervously in agreement, hoping that the fear in their eyes will not give away their weak position.

"Okay—rock, paper, scissors," Slater starts abruptly.

"Hey, wait, I wasn't ready, Slater," Graham squeals.

"Are you ready now, runt?"

Graham is trying to mind read which hand gesture Slater will throw out first. So, Graham begins with the rock. "Ro-sham-bo—rock," Graham says at the same time Slater shows a rock too.

"Go again," Slater says. "Ro-sham-bo—rock," Slater says, throwing his hands in the air. "Rock smashes scissors, Graham! I am the champion once again! We call Martian's Landing, squirt."

Graham looks at Slater and all of Slater's fifth-grade friends as they trail off into the most mysterious part of the park that Slater and Graham discovered together years ago with their dad. The leafy canopy widely extending over the sloped ground beneath can only be explained as a parking garage for an alien spaceship. Graham can't wait to be one of the big kids so he can do whatever he wants, like Slater.

"Oh well. You guys wanna go follow the brook until we get to Two Tall Trees?" Graham says, pretending to his friends that following the brook will make this part of the adventure even cooler since it's technically off-limits.

"Yeah, let's go get some sticks and we can play *old man in the woods who keeps falling down*," Grady Zelner says to the group.

Grady is the ham of third grade. He never needs music or fancy dance clothes to hold the attention of the audience on talent show night; he just acts out scenes from plays he has been writing since second grade. His favorite is to play the character of a little old man who keeps falling down dramatically, and the way Grady rolls around like a turtle on its back has everyone in stitches. No one knows where he gets his ideas from, but this is how he entertains his friends.

"Okay, but do not even think of pushing me in the water when you fall down, Grady," Cooper Varney warns. "Because my mom will be so mad if I come home soaking wet like last time when we went fishing and you pulled me in by pretending to be a fish on the end of my line. Not funny, Grady. Still mad at you, dude," Cooper says with a wicked smile.

"I promise not to get you wet this time. Hey, Dante, can you still do your scary animal noises?" Graham asks the shyest boy in their group.

Dante Marcus is brilliant at impersonating lions and anything else that roars, along with elephants and wild monkeys. He's working on birds right now, but he says he can only do a mynah bird, which sounds just like a human really, so where's the real challenge in that?

"Everybody, get a stick. We'll do sword fights first, then we'll walk along the brook on our way to Two Tall Trees," Graham says excitedly, picking up the first perfect walking stick that has bumps along its sides from knots bulging on the wood. It is almost as tall as Graham, but not too heavy for lugging. "Here's mine. Probably it belonged to some old man needing a cane for the woods, but then—why did he leave it behind?"

"Ooh, maybe he fell in the brook and was swept away to the waterfall at the end," Dante says conspiratorially.

"No, wait, maybe he found an abandoned canoe to float down the brook, but there was no room for his stick because he already had two oars," Jason Hamigachi chimes in eagerly.

Jason is bigger than the rest of the third graders. His mother says he comes from a family of sumo wrestlers on his grandfather's side, so everyone grows up to be big and strong. At school, everyone gathers around Jason at lunch to see what his mother has packed for him. Sometimes he will do trades if his mother has made her famous spider sushi rolls. On these lucky days, everyone offers up their best toys, desserts, or video games for keeps.

"I got it—maybe he was kidnapped by mountain people and all he could leave behind was this stick as a clue that he was here," Graham offers.

"Quick, are there any initials carved into the side of your stick?" Jason asks frantically.

"Wait, look for any scratches that spell out the word H-E-L-P or S-O-S, which is navy code for save our ship," Cooper says, rushing toward the stick to inspect it himself.

"Nope, nothing here. You guys go find your own sticks. We're almost to Two Trees and we haven't gotten to the bend in the brook yet," Graham says, sounding like a little colonel in charge.

The boys walk deeper through the forest looking for twigs suitable for swordplay—too thick and it will be difficult to whip your opponent; too flimsy and it will not be a good defender. The brook babbles on and the forest grows thicker until the shadows of the Two Tall Trees hover at the end of the wooded grove. Only the boulders and caves ahead can lure them outside of their boundaries. The boys feel chilled from the late afternoon shade, which reminds them time is fleeting before their first check-in. But they have come this far, so they decide to make a run for the mountain beyond Two Tall Trees.

"Hey, guys, let's take the shortcut Slater and I found a long time ago up through the backside of the mountain," Graham says without waiting for a group consensus.

The boys wind their way around the steeper side of the mountain still suitable for hikers but carved with a narrow dirt path and plenty of rock ridges to grab for balance.

"Can we get to the top before we need to go back?" Dante asks, assuming someone with a watch will know. He is the only one among his friends who still cannot tell time. His mother insists that he learn it on the old-fashioned clocks with the hour and the minute hands and refuses to buy him a digital watch like all of his friends.

"I've done this like a hundred times before, and I am pretty sure we can get to the top and back down before our dads expect us," Graham says assuredly.

Without a worry in the world, the boys carry on with made-up stories about hikers who lost their way in these parts and got stuck on this mountain overnight. Their bodies were never seen again until a Scout troop sleeping at the base of Two Tall Trees Mountain swore they were awakened with the image of three ghosts dressed in plaid lumberjack shirts.

"Stop it, you guys," Jason Hamigachi says with a quivering voice. "You know I don't like ghost stories."

"Aw, we're just playing around. Hey, watch me—who am I?" Grady asks, hoping to distract the tears that look like they might be forming in Jason's eyes. Grady rolls around on his back as the little old man who has helplessly fallen and can't get up. For some reason, this gets a laugh every time. He wriggles his legs and arms to roll side to side, trying to gain some momentum to prop himself up. The boys start laughing again and forget all about the ghosts that they completely made up.

They finally make it up to the peak of the mountain one mile from its base. A full shadow is cast over the top of the hill from the surrounding pine and oak trees. Their limbs blocking the rays of light make it seem much later than it is.

"Hey, let's play hide-and-seek before we have to head back," Cooper says, hoping the others are just as willing.

"Okay, but I don't want to be it," Dante says firmly as he now remembers crevices he spotted on the way up the hill that he could easily fit inside if he stood real still. Nobody would ever find him.

"I don't want to be it either," Graham calls.

"Not me. Ha-ha, Jason, you're it," Grady says mockingly, scurrying over to the other boys.

"I don't want to be it either," Jason says feebly.

"Well, *we're* all hiding first, so when *you* find one of us, then you can hide too," Graham says, hoping this sounds fair enough to Jason.

"Okay, I'm only counting to twenty and then—" Jason gets interrupted by the mutiny.

"No, you gotta count to a hundred. Those are the rules. We can't hide real good if you don't give us enough time to find our perfect spot," Cooper states passionately.

"Yeah, you gotta give us the correct amount of time, Jason. Just count to a hundred and then you can come look for us," Grady agrees.

"Well, where is off-limits?" Jason asks.

"Okay, halfway down the mountain is off-limits. Stay above the poison oak bushes," Graham says, reminding them where those red-leafed plants were that they tried to avoid touching with their spear sticks on the way up the hill.

"And that counts for the backside of the mountain, too—we can go on the opposite side, but not more than halfway down, all right, everybody?" Grady explains.

"All right, I'm starting to count right now, and I'm not counting slowly." Jason puts his head toward the side of the mountain, burrowing his face into his elbow, and shouts, "One, two, three—" His voice trails off as the boys scatter.

Immediately a skirmish of feet runs in directions away from one another, especially away from Jason, and then he hears the sounds of even more frantic shuffling after changing directions at the last minute.

"Ninety-one, ninety-two, ninety-three," Jason says diligently.

Just as the group hears ninety-six being called, Dante decides to throw out some wild roars in the direction of where the other boys are located, as if this is where he himself is positioned.

Jason hears the lion's call clear as day and knows exactly which way to head so he can end this game quickly. "Ninety-nine, one-hundred. Ready or not, here I come."

Bushes rustle as Jason uses his old man stick to poke through anything big enough to hide an eight-year-old. None of his friends are as big as he is, so he spears into the tiniest of empty rabbit holes and whacks against trees, hoping to scare his friends possibly hiding behind one.

With each step, Jason approaches the mountain with growing fear. For some reason, it seems very, very still out here. "I'm coming for you. Better not laugh or you'll give yourself away," Jason says, hoping they will make some kind of sound to give up their spot.

Graham has found the perfect place—a dark cavern hollowed out of one side of this mountain. The last time he and Slater came upon it by accident, it seemed so much smaller. Right now, he can back up several feet and still see the ground well enough because the light coming in from the mouth of the opening has not yet faded. He remembers that the ground here is not solid and that he and Slater were able to slide easily on the wet mud packed into the floor.

"Where are you? Time to come out from wherever you are," Jason sings at the top of his lungs.

Just as Graham takes one more step backward into the shadows, hoping Jason does not catch a glimpse of him, his foot plants unevenly on something that feels like a branch root growing from the ground. In the same split second Graham realizes there are no trees growing inside caves, a hand attached to the body that is attached to the foot that Graham is now standing on swiftly covers Graham's mouth. A panic shoots through Graham's heart as a belt is tied around his stomach, keeping his arms secured at his sides while a blindfold is clumsily tied around his head to cover his eyes. The hand covering his mouth smells familiar—sulfur, the smell you detect after lighting matches.

"I'm getting closer," Jason says hopefully. "I can see your elbow and your big butt sticking out Cooper Varney."

Cooper hopes this is just a ruse. He thinks the blanket of leafy branches he has tucked himself beneath is a pretty good cover. Carefully, he listens. He hears no footsteps. He is actually pretty comfortable and could even take a nap if it weren't for the fly that keeps buzzing his ears.

"Ah, ha! I've got you, Cooper Varney! I told you I could see your butt," Jason says so gleefully, thrilled that he is not the lone man out anymore.

"Aw, man, I thought I had myself hidden real good, too."

"Umm, Coop, if I were you, I would get out of here pretty fast," Jason says, backing away slowly. "You've got a dormant hornet's nest on your back!"

"Get it off! Help me get it off! I thought it was just a fly," Cooper screams hysterically because he hates bees of any kind.

This is exactly what Jason was hoping to avoid because a dormant hive is not the kind of enemy he wants to awaken. "Dude, just get out from that pile of branches and run over here," Jason says, convinced his plan will work.

"We got to get outta here," Cooper screams some more.

He runs wildly with his arms flailing all around above his head, hoping this will be enough to ward off any bee attacks. He runs downhill and looks back only to be sure that Jason is trailing him closely. The two hightail it together to the base of Two Tall Trees Mountain in their fastest time of twelve minutes. They run the rest of the way along the brook and over to Wild Clover to find their dads—and only then do they remember the game they left behind.

"Dad, Dad, we were in the middle of a bee attack with, like, a hundred bees chasing us on Two Trees!" Cooper exclaims to his father.

"Yeah, Dad, you should have seen them. They were like all over Cooper's back and circling his head and trying to get inside his ears and everything!" Jason continues, filling in the rest with his elaborate details.

"Boys, what were you doing near a bee's nest?" Martin Varney asks.

"We were hiding and I was under the branches and I thought it was a fly and it just kept buzzing," Cooper says, trying to make more sense for his father.

"Yeah, Mr. Varney, it was like a big hornet's nest with them all still asleep except for like a few that were angry," Jason says, proudly recalling what he has learned in science about bees, honey, nests, and hives.

"Okay, okay, well we're glad you guys are all right then. Sounds like you were pretty brave planning your escape," Daniel Hamigachi says with a chuckle.

"Where are the other boys? They right behind you? Or in the bathrooms?" Hank Hannigan asks.

"Umm, they're still up on the mountain because we had to leave on account of the killer bees." Cooper turns to his own father to continue, "So we just ran, Dad. We ran as fast as we could so we could come tell you." He rests his palms on his knees, bending over to catch his breath.

"Boys, you know you're not supposed to leave your buddies behind. Are the other kids still together?" Martin Varney asks, a bit more worried this time.

"I know, but we just had to escape from the killer bees," Cooper says, convinced that the bee excuse is pretty valid.

"Jason, are your friends still together on Two Trees?" Daniel Hamigachi asks, holding both of Jason's biceps as he kneels down to look his son in the eyes.

"Yeah, we're playing hide-and-seek," Jason says. "I was finding everybody and I found Cooper first because I saw his big butt sticking out." Jason throws a wide-eyed smile to Cooper.

"Do you think we need to go up there and get them?" Daniel says, looking to Hank and Martin.

"I guess if they're still together, they've got another fifteen minutes before check-in," Hank says logically.

"Okay, let's just let them have their fun and see who makes it down first," Martin says, completely satisfied that at least his son is back in time to work on his third hot dog.

Meanwhile, the game of hide-and-seek is still in progress. However, there is a new dilemma. Dante has the terrible realization that the tree he has so skillfully climbed up is now a bit too high to climb down. He does not want to give away his position yet, so he quietly sends some birdcalls to Grady nearby. Maybe *he* can offer Dante a hand out of the tree without both of them getting caught by Jason.

"Cuc-koo, cuc-koo," Dante calls with a convincing pause between syllables the way a real bird would. *Where is everybody?* he wonders. Nobody responds. In fact, it occurs to Dante that he has heard nothing but silence for a while now. Not even Jason Hamigachi has been calling out "olly olly oxen free" like he should if he wants to end this game.

Meanwhile, back in the cave, Graham struggles to get free from his captors.

"Le-me-go, le-me-go," Graham manages to say through muzzled hands cupped over his mouth. His voice is muffled and unable to reach beyond the cave walls for anyone outside to hear.

"What should we do with him?" a deep voice asks.

"We're gonna tie him to that rock and leave him here for the bats to find tonight," a second gruff voice says with a commanding presence—perhaps disguised so Graham will not be able to identify them to the police.

"Help! Le-me-go! Help someone, help!" Graham screams as loud as he can through tight fingers clasped securely around the lower half of his face.

"Kid, you should have known this was coming," says the eerily croaky voice of the second man who suddenly knocks Graham to the ground and sits on him to tickle him under his arms and across his ribs. Graham hates this more than anything because he laughs so hard his eyes start tearing up.

"Slaaaaa-ter!" Graham is finally free to scream his brother's name. "You scared me half to death, you stupid," Graham says. Tears from his ticklefest drip down his cheeks.

"I told you, when you least expect it, expect it!" Slater says, high-fiving his buddies Macaroni and Phil. "I got you good this time. You should have seen the look on your face," Slater says, laughing with pride.

"How'd you even know we were up here?" Graham asks, still trying to get over his scare.

"We totally followed you guys and you had no idea. Once we saw you heading for Two Trees, we ran up the front trail when you took the backside to the cave," Slater says, dusting off his pants.

"Man, that was a good one, Slater," Phil says, pretty proud of himself for his part in the play-acting.

"Okay, we ready? Check-in is in about five minutes. We're gonna be late anyway," Macaroni says eagerly.

"Yeah, let's go. We've had our fun for today," Slater says, wrapping his arm around Graham and pulling him into his stinky armpit.

"Slater, I still hate you. You guys are all mean," Graham says with mock anger.

"Oh yeah, we'll see what happens when I chase you down the hill. Last one to the bottom sits in the backseat this time," Slater calls back to Graham while running full speed ahead, kicking up dust behind him and nearly stumbling a time or two on the rocks chipped from the side of the mountain.

"Hey, you guys, wait for me," Graham says nervously. Anxious to not be left behind, he runs as quickly as he can while the forest sun begins to set, hastening the glowing dusk.

With Phil Moore and Macaroni Maroney in tow, all four boys stumble and slide their way to the bottom of the hill as fast as they possibly can. Just another stretch along the brook and, with the good fortune that nobody running this fast has accidentally fallen in, they make it to Wild Clover—within the ten minutes late rule before you really get in big trouble.

"We're here, we made it, we're not that late, Dad," Slater says, panting for breath as he checks in. Graham is at his side, and both boys huff as if they have been running around the track for miles. "I was here first, Dad, so I call shotgun for the ride home," he finishes and then makes a face to Graham as a reminder of what happens when you do not show respect to the oldest kid in the family.

"Yeah, Dad, we made it and I don't even care. Slater can sit up front for the rest of the week," Graham relents.

"Wow, seems like you guys had a pretty good time today with each other, I'm happy to hear that," Hank says, rubbing both of their heads with his gorilla paws.

"Everybody here? Who's missing a buddy?" the dads ask as they look for each of their sons.

"Hey, boys, where's Dante?" Jim Marcus asks the crowd of youngsters about his son.

"And where's Grady?" Doctor Zelner asks, putting on his glasses to see if someone is coming from the direction of the brook.

"They were buddies together. We haven't seen them," one of the other third graders offers. "We were playing on the Big Willow field the whole time."

"Who saw Dante and Grady last?" Doctor Zelner rushes to ask.

"We were playing with them, but I think we left them up on Two Tall Trees Mountain because we were in the middle of hide-and-seek," Graham says, realizing he can't explain why they abandoned the game without all of their friends intact.

"Yeah, they must still be in their hiding spots," Jason confirms.

"Why did you guys leave them up there alone?" Hank asks a bit sternly.

"We didn't do it on purpose, Dad. It's just that we wanted to get back before the check-in time so we didn't get in trouble," Graham says, nearly on the verge of tears because he does not like to be in trouble with his dad.

"Guys, let's go. Show us where you were hiding," Jim Marcus says calmly, but he's obviously in a hurry to find his son now that the days are getting shorter and darkness comes so quickly.

"Hank, who is staying here with the boys?" Doctor Zelner asks, putting some bottles of water in his backpack.

Hank Hannigan sounds in command as he makes a plan. "I'd like to go with you guys. Roger, will you and Evan and Daniel stay here with the rest of the boys and be sure they stay only on Wild Clover or Big Willow from this point out?" This reminds them all it is good to have a friend in law enforcement. Nothing bad can happen when you have a guy around whose job it is to protect everyone else.

As the fathers charge up Two Tall Trees Mountain with their sons following close behind for their second time today, voices carry with urgent calls for the two missing boys.

"Daaaaaan-teeeee! Graaaa-dy! Where are you?" Doctor Zelner shouts in every direction.

"Olly olly oxen free," Graham and his little friends shout out, signaling to Dante and Marcus that it is safe to reappear.

"Hey, I'm up here! Hey, Daaaad!" Dante calls cheerfully, seeing that his father has finally come to his rescue.

"Son, what are you doing up in that tree?"

"Dad, I had the best hiding spot. Nobody could find me forever, but I think I'm too high," Dante says with a big grin on his face, so proud of the fact that he thought of climbing up like a bird or a monkey before anyone else did.

"Dante, just hold on to those branches real tight, son, and we're going to get you down in just a minute," Jim Marcus says, bemused because he remembers finding himself in worse situations when he was even younger than Dante.

While the other fathers give Jim a boost and stand guard below, ready to catch Dante if he falls out of the tree, Doctor Zelner still calls around for Grady.

"Graaaa-dy, where are you?" he yells nervously as faint echoes drive softly through the woods.

"Graaaa-dy, olly olly oxen free," Jason Hamigachi shouts loudly. "It's safe to come out now, the game's over."

With Dante out of the tree and his father Jim grateful to know his son is in one piece, they join forces with the others who have gotten no response from Grady.

"Dad, I know! I know where Grady is probably hiding," Graham says excitedly, convinced he knows right where to look. "There's a berry bush this way. I know Grady was saying he was hungry; he probably wanted to go find that berry bush."

Lo and behold—sleeping behind this mulberry bush is an eight-year-old boy snoring away. The smears of dark purple around the corners of his lips indicate that he did indeed find the berries to be delicious. How many he ate would be the tale he would later tell, but for now it is time to carry him down to Wild Clover before the sun falls behind the mountain. This will remain a constant memory for the families who attended father-son day at Willow Glenn. Unfortunately, next year will be full of other events that will prevent them from meeting together as friends again.

CHAPTER 9

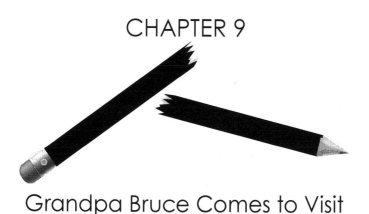

Grandpa Bruce Comes to Visit

Only in this serene neighborhood, where tree-lined streets are dotted by colorful houses resembling a painter's palette of sherberts can a surprising noise be heard—the kind that startles and jolts neighbors from their deep slumber. Amid the morning glow of the amber sun rolling in through the cracks of kitchen windows, a ferocious snarl sounds from across the street. A simple boy dressed in his favorite green sweatshirt, the color of muddied lily pads from the pond nearby, whistles a happy tune. Its high, melodious pitch, however, unearths the overweight Old English bulldog from his nap. The dog races to meet his enemy at the fence line, and all the while, slobber reels in the wind behind him.

Slater uses the tip of his bat to bang rhythmically along the boards of the short picket fence. This is his usual pattern whenever he walks to Macaroni's house for his ride to school on the days when Lynn

Hannigan has to drive into her city office to do presentations for her boss or clients. As a hotel decorator, she has a lot of important reasons to be away from home even though she says the two biggest reasons to work from the house are Slater and Graham.

Meanwhile in Mrs. Maroney's carpool, her son Macaroni, Phil Moore, and Slater figure out ways Slater can earn that pie money for the Thanksgiving Pie Challenge coming in two weeks.

Without using too many words, the boys have worked out a code to use around any adults so nobody is the wiser to their plans. "Macaroni, have you checked?" Slater asks, as if Macaroni should remember this means he was supposed to check his special money box under his bed for how much of his own allowance he has stashed away that he can contribute to Slater's $300 goal.

"Not even half of half," Macaroni says slyly. He watches Slater and Phil do the mental math, and since neither one of them agree on what the final number is without working it out on paper first or using a calculator, which is their preference, Macaroni solves the equation. "Barry Zito—Giants *and* As."

"Okay, why didn't you say so sooner?" Slater says, exasperated, as if this could have saved a lot of time.

They have memorized the jersey numbers to all of their favorite MLB players so whenever they need a quick answer on a math test, someone is bound to call out a player's name disguised as a cough.

So, now that they know Macaroni only has $75 saved, the other two boys chime in with their amounts. Phil says, "Uh, Joe DiMaggio,

Yankees. Sorry guys, my mom just had a birthday and my dad said I was old enough to pick out something nice with my own money."

"What? You only have five dollars? Come on, you spend more than that at the ice cream truck after school, Phil. How much you really got?" Slater says, drilling him because he knows Phil is stingy.

"Look, I can't even go into my other place—it's off limits, and you know it."

His *other* place is a beautiful porcelain doll his grandmother gave him for his fifth birthday. She had been expecting Phil to be a little girl, but he surprised everyone when he was born. The doll had been her own mother's, and she wanted to pass it down to her great-granddaughter.

The doll is built with a secret plug hidden behind the bow on her back just above her wide belle skirt. After you untie it and pull out the plug, you can empty the entire contents of money grandma has stuffed inside for Phil's first five years of life. When she gave it to him, she told him that even though he was a little boy, if he took good care to put his birthday money and Christmas money in his doll, then he would be as rich as a princess someday.

While he does not wish to be a princess someday, he does love that this life-size doll, which stands as tall as his knee, is already half stuffed. So he was happy to keep the doll, but he made a few changes to it. He got an old eye patch from when his grandfather had cataract surgery and put it over her face. He drew a little curly moustache above her lip and found a parrot off of an old key chain and taped it to her shoulder. This little pirate is going to give him enough booty to pay for college someday—or to buy his first hot rod car when he turns sixteen. He hasn't decided yet.

"Aww, man, you are so greedy. Do you even know how much you've got in there?" Slater says, trying to intimidate Phil into giving up some of his loot.

"Look," Phil says, kind of whispering now because he can see Mrs. Maroney watching them from her rearview mirror, "it's not the kind of thing I'm supposed to talk about. Besides, my mom says that if I ever need bail money, that's the first place she's looking."

They both laugh easily at this one because his mother does not like Phil's attitude after he comes back from visiting his father when it's his turn for custody weekends.

"What about you, Slater? Who's your player?" Macaroni quizzes Slater to see if he even has enough to buy *one* pie, let alone trying to raise enough money for three.

"Hank Aaron and A-Rod," Slater says semiconfidently.

"Please tell me from when A-Rod was with the Yankees," Macaroni says, hoping this will secure a few more bucks.

"Yes, from when he was with the Yankees," Slater says as if it should have been obvious.

The boys feel pretty comfortable that Macaroni's mom has not yet figured out what the heck they are talking about entirely. But at least they now know they can for sure afford one Thanksgiving pie with a combined $119 coming from Slater's $44 for Hank Aaron plus $13 from Alex Rodriguez on the Yankees, and Phil's pittance of $5—Joe DiMaggio would be insulted to know how little his name was worth in this conversation—and Macaroni's $75.

"Hey, if I'm putting in the most, then I should be the one who gets to throw the pie," Macaroni says logically.

"No way. The whole point is I am going to throw the pie at Miss Burbank. I can't wait to see the look on her face, too, she hates me so bad," Slater says with an evil grin.

"Dude, she does hate you, it's so obvious," Macaroni agrees in solidarity.

"What'd you ever do to her anyway?" Phil asks innocently since he transferred here late and has little idea about the fourth-grade battles waged between Miss Burbank and Slater Hannigan.

"Oh, man, you have no idea. I think it peaked when you made her cry, right, Slater?" Macaroni says, trying to think back to how it all started.

"She did, too. She cried right in front of the whole class, it was so funny," Slater says, smiling.

"Like, a little, or a lot?" Phil wants to know.

"Like, she kept trying to say why she was so mad and her words came out all screechy and garbled and we all just sat their frozen because she was such a mess," Slater recounts for Phil.

"Yeah, I can't remember what set her off. It just came out of some random place. She kept trying to say, 'Slaaaa-ter, this is on youuuu,' but she was crying too hard to make any sense. Thank goodness it was almost time to go and then the bell finally rang. She got a sub the next day, and when she returned, she never said a word."

Macaroni fills in the blanks for Phil who stares at Slater like he is half hero and half king of torturers. Phil never saw anything like this in his last school.

"Yeah, she's got it in for me for sure this year. I don't even have to be guilty, I already know she wants me out of her class," Slater admits. "But then I wouldn't get to hang with you guys as much, so I promised my mom I would really try."

"That's cool," Phil says, trying to figure out what he makes of this story anyway.

"Um, are you forgetting that the whole point was for us to get *three* pies?" Macaroni says quickly to remind them that he wants his very own.

"Actually, dudes, it's only special rules for us if we come up with $300. That girl from student council said we could probably get some extra pies only then, but we gotta get the money first. Money talks," Phil says with authority.

He must have picked this saying up from his dad who is some big businessman. Every other weekend after seeing his dad, Phil has some new phrase he likes to toss around to look like a big shot. He's not fooling anyone, though, with this tough guy act. Macaroni and Slater have seen him cry before. In fact, they have all seen each other cry before. And this is the bond that remains unbroken between them because nobody else needs to know what reduced each one of them to tears last year.

"Boys, here we go. Jump out, have a great day at school," Mrs. Maroney says sweetly after flipping up the child safety locks on all of the doors. "Macaroni, come back here for a minute," she says with that sweet, charming voice of hers.

"Mom, I'm gonna be late," Macaroni says impatiently, dutifully walking one step toward the car that he had nearly made a clean getaway from.

"Give me a kiss good-bye, darling. You're still Momma's precious, even though you are getting to be so big," Mrs. Maroney says, reaching her hands up to grab Macaroni's face, squeezing his cheeks and rubbing his nose with hers.

"Awww, Mom, everyone's looking. Let me go. I'll see you after school," Macaroni says, completely mortified that his mom still insists on kissing him good-bye in front of the drop-off every single time she drives carpool.

After shifting the car into drive, she pulls away slowly, rolling down the electric car window and calling out enthusiastically behind Macaroni, "I love you, my sweetheart."

In the same split second he thinks he can avoid her unwanted attention—because lots of kids are called sweetheart and no one will know it's directed toward him if he doesn't turn around to acknowledge her—his mom adds, "Have a good day, my noodle, Macaroni!" and toots her horn in a friendly manner.

Slater and Phil are waiting by the front doors of Esther Bookman Elementary busting a gut because Macaroni has heart-shaped lipstick on his cheek from where his mother kissed him.

"Your mom loooooves youuuu," Phil teases.

"That's exactly how my mom treats Graham because he's the baaaaby too," Slater chimes in.

"You guys knock it off. See if I give you any of my money, Slater." Macaroni stomps off in a huff to their room number line.

"We're just joking around, Macaroni. Swear, we didn't mean anything by it. It's just kinda so sweet, right Phil?" Slater says, looking to Phil to help him out of this hole.

"Yeah, we're just messing with you, dude. We would totally die, too, if that was our mom," Phil assures him with a look of trust that Macaroni believes. "We good?"

"Whatever—you guys are hateful sometimes," Macaroni says with a wisecracking smile, "but, still not sure I'm giving you all of my $75. Slater, you gotta figure out a better way," Macaroni says—and *now* he feels better about accepting their apology.

Within the first fifteen minutes during today's class warm-up for math boosters, the girls from student council return to remind Miss Burbank's class that there are only two weeks left to collect pie challenge money. "If your class raises $100, you will get to pie Miss Burbank, and don't forget, Miss Burbank, we're going to give you a beautiful pumpkin pie to take home for your holiday celebrations," the girls say warmly before stepping toward the exit door.

"Girls, remind us, when is the deadline for collections. Is it tomorrow?" Miss Burbank says, hoping everyone has already forgotten about it and will miss the deadline.

"Oh, no, Miss Burbank, your class still has plenty of time to earn money. We won't collect your envelope until a week from Friday, so turn over those piggy banks, everybody, and remember this is for a good cause. We all want to get the yearbook for a discount, right?" Charity says as she looks boldly around the room, wondering why the boys in the back are laughing now.

"I have a question," Slater says, raising his hand and awaiting Miss Burbank's permission to speak further.

"Yes, Slater, what is it?" Miss Burbank replies begrudgingly, wondering if she is going to regret this.

"Do you guys remember how you said there would be a *special* prize if we earned enough for three pies?" Slater says, trying to jog their memory.

"Are you really planning to raise $300, Slater? That would be so fantastic for the whole school. It would really go a long way to help meet our goal of getting every single student a discount. Do you think you can do it?" Charity Bronstein asks excitedly.

"Well, I don't know yet, but I wanted to make sure you were prepared because I think you guys promised us three pies if we do," Slater says confidently, trying to negotiate this deal before he even has his end of the bargain supplied.

"Okay, girls, thanks for stopping by," Miss Burbank says swiftly, trying to shoo the student council representatives out the door and get her class to stop thinking about pies and to start thinking about math.

✏ ✏ ✏ ✏

After school, Slater has a pretty nice surprise himself waiting for him at home. Grandpa Bruce has come for a short visit to see his only son and his two favorite grandsons.

"Grandpa, Grandpa, I didn't know you were coming to town," Slater says in a rush as he drops his backpack and runs into the living room to squeeze the only Grandpa he's ever known.

"Aww, Slater, I'm so happy to see you too, son." Grandpa Bruce holds him tightly before pushing him away for a small second to get a better look into those brown eyes. "You are growing bigger every time I see you. It's been since Easter, and look at you now. I can't call you my *little* grandson anymore, can I?"

"Naw, I'm not the biggest in my class this year, but I'm not the smallest, that's for sure," Slater rattles on excitedly. "And Gramps, I'm hitting this season, you should see me, it's like I'm on fire," Slater continues with all of his great news.

"Son, that's pretty impressive. Before you know it, you'll be in the Pony League and scouts will be coming to know you by name. You've got talent, boy, real talent. Can't train talent, that's for sure," Grandpa Bruce says proudly. "That's why I survived the military. Pure talent, they said, and the good head on my shoulders."

"Hi, Bruce," Lynn calls through the door, just now coming home from her day of meetings in the city.

"Mom, look. Grandpa surprised us," Slater says cheerily.

"Well, your father and I knew, but we thought it'd be more fun this way to keep it a secret from you and Graham," she says, taking off her trench coat. She shakes it robustly, sliding her hand firmly across the backside to straighten out any wrinkles, and then hangs it over the dining room chair before waltzing toward Grandpa Bruce to give him a hug.

"Grandpa, you're here, you're here," Graham says as he comes bounding in from where the school bus has just dropped him off outside. He's lucky—he gets to ride the bus. Since there is not enough money to transport all grade levels to Esther Bookman Elementary, the district negotiated for a few busses to deliver only the lower grades home; fourth and fifth graders have to hoof it or find their own rides.

"Here I am, squirt! Run and jump!" Grandpa says heartily as he leans his broad frame forward ready to greet Graham and scoop him up into his arms, hoisting him high above his head so Graham can feel like he is flying, if only for a minute.

"Grandpa! Grandpa! I can't believe you're here!" Graham squeals. Seeing Grandpa is even better than coming home to a puppy.

"Okay, Grandpa puts you down now, Graham. You are getting bigger, too! But, still not too big to go flying in the air with your Grandpa—right, Big Mac?"

"Right!" Graham says heartily. Big Mac is the nickname he earned because whenever he would play at the park with Grandpa or go fishing with Grandpa and Slater, Graham could always finish two whole Big Macs by himself. Nobody understands how he manages to stay rail thin after eating so much.

"Lynn, I suppose I have time to visit with the boys in their rooms before we need to wash up for dinner?" Grandpa Bruce asks gently.

"Oh, you have plenty of time. When your son gets home, he is taking us all out to dinner to celebrate your arrival. Italian, everybody," Lynn says, smiling hopefully.

"Oh, sure, I can eat Italian. I think that's a good suggestion. Then I have just the right amount of time I need with these two soldiers of mine," Grandpa Bruce says affectionately.

The two boys and Grandpa Bruce bound up the stairs to Graham's room first. "Grandpa, Grandpa, I want to show you something," Graham says secretly, holding his grandfather's big hand bulging with blue veins and knotted fingers. "Look, my fish just had babies," Graham says, carting Grandpa to peer inside his aquarium with the most amazing phosphorous blue light that looks like a deep sapphire brightly cast behind the dozens of tiny goldfish.

"Well, I'll be," Grandpa says, peeking over Graham's shoulder. "You sure do have a lot of fish in here, that's for sure, Graham. Plenty beautiful, too," he says, tussling Graham's hair which has grown long again since the beginning-of-the-school-year cut in August.

"Tell me, what other things are exciting in your life, and how is school going?" Grandpa sits and listens while Graham yammers on and on about each of his friends and how much he likes his teacher this year and how he's glad he doesn't have a lady teacher because this man teacher seems to know how to reach boys, at least this is what his mom says all of the time. Graham continues with his wish list for a puppy for Christmas and talks about the stories he likes to read and all of the things he might like to be when he grows up.

Grandpa listens intently to this hour-long monologue that really requires no audience at all because Graham can just talk and talk and talk and has always been this way, even if nobody is around to play with him. He is comfortable entertaining himself. His parents always say this is the surest sign of a gifted child.

"Graham, you are growing up to be a real fine boy. I'm so proud of you, and I know your grandmother would find you to be very special if she were still with us today."

"Yep, I know you're sad, Grandpa, but don't worry, Grandma is your angel now," Graham says warmly and nuzzles his head into his grandfather's neck while squeezing him tight.

"You're a good boy; thank you for the hug."

"Slater, what about you? What's doing with you at school this year? And tell me more about your season. We always knew you would grow up to be strong like your father," Grandpa Bruce says assuredly and waits for Slater to open up like Graham.

"Well, there's this pie challenge at school to raise money for yearbook discounts for all the kids, and I keep thinking I'd like to help out, but I don't have enough money," Slater says slowly, stopping to see what his Grandpa thinks so far.

"You want to help the whole school get a discount on yearbooks?"

"Well, it's kind of like a fund-raiser. Every class has to see if they can raise $100, but me and my friends want to triple that—" Slater says before he is cut short by his grandpa, who is misinterpreting Slater's intentions.

"Well, son, if it's money you need, I know how you can get some," Grandpa Bruce adds cheerily. "That's a pretty lucky school to have such a generous boy as you trying to help out so much."

"Gee, thanks, Grandpa, I knew I could count on you."

"How about tomorrow after school we go to the park where you like to play, and for every piece of trash you pick up, I'll give you a dollar. When you finish there, if you still don't have enough, we can go downtown to Memorial Park, which is three times as big. What do you say about that?" Grandpa Bruce says, happy to help.

"Well, I wasn't thinking I would be picking up trash," Slater says sheepishly. *What if someone from school sees me picking up trash at the park?*

"Well, son, don't be so proud that you can't make your community shine in any way you can. That's how I raised your father, and look at what he's doing now to rid your town of trash," Grandpa Bruce says with pride over the career path his son has taken as the district attorney responsible for putting away the bad guys.

"Umm, Grandpa, can I bring Macaroni and Phil to help?" Slater asks politely.

"Sure, if each of you can find hearty pieces of trash worth a dollar each, I'll gladly pay it to you hardworking young men."

So, after school for the next two days, Slater, Macaroni, and Phil join Grandpa Bruce at Sugar Ridge Park first and then Memorial

Park on the second day. Together, the boys earn another $150 dollars, bringing their new total to $269, just $31 dollars shy of their $300 goal.

But before the deadline comes due next week, Slater Hannigan thinks of one more way to earn the rest of his money—and it does not involve doing anything good for his community.

CHAPTER 10

Grandpa Goes to the Grocery Store

The next day, Grandpa Bruce obtains special permission to pick the boys up from school and whisk them away for an afternoon of fishing at the pond. It is one of their favorite things to do together, and on the days when the fish don't bite, Grandpa Bruce has been known to stop at the store to buy a trout or two just to impress their mother.

"Grandpa's here, Slater. We're going fishing." Graham clamors for Slater who is approaching quickly in front of the school's parking lot.

"I know, I got the call from the office saying to wait inside, but I knew you would be out here," Slater says, hitting Graham's little backpack.

"Okay, you go check inside, and I'll wait right here for Grandpa," Graham says excitedly. He can hardly stand the three more minutes it will take for Grandpa to make his way through the line of cars picking up their children. Kids sloppily throw themselves into the backs of minivans then hustle out again to retrieve the band instrument they forgot on the curb.

Honk, honk sounds the alto horn on Grandpa's old T-bird. The deep bellow signals to Graham that Grandpa is in the loop waiting his turn to pull up.

Graham waves wildly toward Grandpa at first, then communicates with his tiny index finger pointing high in the air that he will be right back in just one minute.

In a flash, Graham is gone. He runs into the office to call for Slater. "Grandpa's here already, Slater!"

Before either of them can leave, Mrs. Howston asks that their grandfather come inside to sign the boys out.

"I'll do it; he already saw me." Graham rushes past an incoming parent and heads out the double doors. "Grandpa, come inside!" Even in his loudest voice, Graham's shouts cannot be heard over the parking lot noise. He flashes his arms eagerly back and forth from the distance of the front office to where Grandpa is sitting in line ten cars away, signaling for him to come inside.

Grandpa thinks Graham is waving to him, so he happily waves back. This time, Graham uses both hands to communicate quickly before all of the fish go home for the night. He looks like he is swirling the air in front of him, and Grandpa has no idea what Graham is conveying.

"What is taking so long, Graham? How come you're still up on these steps?" Slater asks impatiently.

"I'm trying to tell Grandpa he needs to get out of the car to come over here, but he just keeps waving back at me," Graham says, smiling and still waving.

"Geesh, Graham, we could already be on the road by now. Stay here and I'll go tell Grandpa to park," Slater says, even more annoyed.

"No, I'll go tell Grandpa, and you stay here, Slater," Graham says as he darts away and runs along the curb where twelve cars are still idling. "Grandpa, the office secretary says you need to come in to sign for us. I'm so excited today is our fishing day, Grandpa!"

"Oh boy, that's right, all these new rules. I forgot I have to come inside. Okay, son, step away from the car so I can find a space to park, but it might be around the block because there are no spots open in this lot," Grandpa says, smiling warmly to Graham and to the line monitor as he signals with his indicator that he wants to pull out. Grandpa puts his left arm out the window to prepare everybody that he intends to creep out of the line and carefully across the lot. Fortunately, a lady is leaving just a few cars away and Grandpa slides into her space.

Graham runs to where Grandpa is walking up the steps toward the office hill, grabs his hand, and swings it in a rhythm that keeps time with their feet. "Hey, Jason, this is my Grandpa. We're going fishing today," Graham calls across to the bus line where his friend from class is waiting to go home.

"Cool," Jason shouts back and gives a wave with his hand. It's hard to hear over all of the kids who are negotiating for their place in line when three buses pull up.

"Well, hello, soldier," Grandpa says cheerfully to Slater, patting him on the back.

"Hey, Grandpa, I was going to come get you myself, but then Graham started running. I'll show you who Mrs. Howston is when we go inside," Slater says officially as if he is in charge of this operation now and not Graham.

"Hi, Mrs. Howston. This is my grandpa, Bruce Hannigan," Slater says politely.

"Well, hello, Mr. Hannigan. Sorry to delay your plans by having you stop inside, but we like to know where all of the children are," Mrs. Howston says gently.

"Oh, thank you for your patience. Sometimes I can be a bit forgetful, and I can't believe how many cars there are trailing up your little street here. I'm lucky I got here early because there were already ten cars ahead of me," Grandpa says, signing his name on the form.

"Yes, yes," Mrs. Howston says with a nod. "Ever since our bus funds were cut we have lots more parents driving kids to and from school. It does tend to get a little hectic out there at times," she says sweetly, collecting her clipboard. "You're all set here. You boys have a nice afternoon with your grandpa." Mrs. Howston beams brightly.

"We're going fishing at our favorite pond," Graham blurts out rapidly, grabbing onto his grandpa's hand with a tight grasp and a broad grin as he looks up toward his grandpa's face, wrinkled and tan.

On their way to the car, they stop at the ice cream truck parked right outside of the school. It's the perfect day for rainbow missiles, otter pops, and push cone sundaes, so they order one of each.

"Boys, I don't mind if you eat these in the car. There's nothing sticky that I can't get off of these seats. I've had this old girl for almost a hundred years and she's still good as new," Grandpa chuckles.

"Really? A hundred years! Wow, that's so old Grandpa," Graham says astonished.

"Well, Graham, I don't think she's *really* a hundred years old. I just mean I've had her for a good long time—ever since your dad was a little boy, I suppose," Grandpa recalls cheerfully. "I used to put him on my lap and let him pretend to drive by holding the steering wheel when we were in the driveway."

"Oh, Grandpa, can I sit on your lap, too?" Graham asks, ready to ditch his ice cream in favor of a ride up front.

"No, no Graham," Grandpa says, shaking his head with a smile. "You're much too big for Grandpa's lap now. You're a big strong boy. Your father was just a little baby who could barely walk when we played that game," Grandpa says, joyfully remembering the good times he had as a young father.

"Aww, Grandpa, I wanted to drive with you," Graham says, wiping the rainbow stains of cherry and orange across his wet face with the back of his sleeve.

"Oh, there'll be plenty of time for that, Graham," Grandpa says, looking at Graham's hair blowing straight into his sticky mouth with each bite of his half-eaten larger-than-life popsicle.

As they head away from school, Grandpa decides to make a short stop at the grocery store for some chewing gum, which always helps his concentration. "I'll be right back. You can listen to the radio and finish your ice cream, okay?"

"Okay, Grandpa," Slater says with his entire mouth completely full after sucking out the vanilla ice cream of his push cone.

While Grandpa meanders toward the store and Graham is completely enthralled with his rocket missile in the backseat, Slater operates fast. He shoves the rest of his dessert into his face with one of the biggest bites he has ever taken—except for that time at Macaroni's house when they tried to have their own hot dog eating contest just for fun. Slater could have won, but that huge bite never went *down*—it came *up* instead with the thirty other bites he'd taken just before in a spew that chucked all over Mrs. Maroney's kitchen counter tops.

"Look at me, I'm driving," Slater says, bouncing around in Grandpa's seat, pretending to steer the wheel wildly around corners.

"Hey, that's not fair. I told Grandpa I wanted to drive," Graham complains from the backseat with his missile pop resting on the leather cushion, dripping Kool-Aid colors into the upholstery.

"Graham, you big baby," Slater grumbles, fiddling with the stereo to find the kind of music *he* likes. "Grandpa already said you'll get your chance, like, in about ten years," he continues to tease.

"Slater, when I'm done with this missile pop, it's my turn," Graham says willfully.

"By the looks of that thing, it's gonna melt all over Grandpa's car before you ever finish it," Slater says with a quick backward glance.

"Vrooom, vroom, ehhhhrk, crash, there goes number 17 coming around the corner way too hot. He did not expect my famous move to be the end of him." Slater narrates his imaginary turns in a speedway race no one else can see.

As soon as Slater announces that he is one lap away from the finish line, he fakes a punch to the automatic transmission to pretend to go into a higher throttle. What he does not realize for the span of twenty seconds is that he has kicked Grandpa's car into neutral and is now slowly rolling backward out of the parking stall. What is even worse for poor Slater is that Grandpa took the only spot left at the *top* of this crooked parking lot—so the weight of the car is now picking up momentum down the sharp incline behind them.

"Slater, what'd you do? Are you really driving this thing?" Graham says in a state of confusion. "You better stop it; we're rolling!" The panic rises in his high-pitched voice. "How do you stop it, Slater?"

"I don't know! It just started moving on its own. There must be a switch," Slater says, equally confused.

In his haste to fix this before Grandpa returns, Slater pushes levers to find anything that will stop the rolling.

"Aaargh, you're getting me wet," Graham says, wiping his face from the spray of the window wipers that are now spewing water across the windshield.

"Help! Can you find my grandpa?" Slater shouts out to the only other lady in the parking lot who is pushing her cart across the lane in front of Slater.

By now, the heavy back end of the car is beginning to catch its rhythm, and what was once a slow, gentle crawl has become more of a push backward like on a swing set. The bad part is that gravity is sucking the car toward the other parked cars behind it and the only hope is that someone can save Slater and Graham before they crunch into the parked minivan nearby.

"Help, Grandpa, help!" Slater shouts wildly while Graham holds onto the neck rest behind Slater's head, preparing for the coming bump.

"Hang on, boys, Grandpa's coming," Grandpa says, toddling as fast as his old feet can carry him.

Fortunately, the store manager is already sprinting ahead of Grandpa. He can see the tail end of Grandpa's Ford Thunderbird closing in on the minivan in its direct path with cartoon stickers all over the window of how many kids and pets are in this family. The caption next to the images of three girls, two small boys, two dogs, and one cat reads, "And one exhausted mom." Beneath that, the frame around the license plate reads, "Golf Widow."

In the nick of time, Bud Donovan, the middle-aged frumpy store manager who once knew how to slide into third base about forty years ago in Little League, dives over the driver's door to grasp the emergency brake hard, yanking it clear toward the sky in one sturdy move.

The car comes to a sudden stop. Bud shifts the gear stick from neutral to park and hangs on the doorframe for the minute he contemplates how much of his belly is smashing into Slater, the underage driver.

"You saved us! Thank you, sir," Graham shouts from the backseat, clapping his hands.

"Thanks, mister. I'm sure I would have found that stick, but I didn't know what it was for," Slater says sheepishly.

Bud Donovan pushes off from the dashboard and slides his belly backward to stand upright again. As he readjusts his uniform shirt, tucking it into his trousers, and feels for his name tag above his breast pocket, he says finally, "Boys, this could have been a real serious accident. That would have been a charge your parents would have to pay if there was injury done to another person or damage to a car."

"Boys," Grandpa says, sounding worried and relieved all in the same breath, "what happened here?"

Graham is the first to chime in with all of the details of Slater's racecar driving and putting his sticky hands all over the wheel and then pretending to go fast while playing with the gears.

"Gee, thanks, Graham," Slater says sarcastically. "I think Grandpa is smart enough to know that I didn't do it on purpose."

"Slater, trouble does have a way of following you, son," Grandpa says, staring at Slater still sitting behind the wheel, neither one of them quite sure what to do next.

"Thank you, sir," Grandpa says to the manager, glancing at the name tag that reads Bud Donovan, Store 55 Manager. "Bud, I appreciate your help here today. I didn't know if I would be able to get to the car as fast as you did, not with these old feet," Grandpa says, humbly grateful.

"Think nothing of it. Sometimes these things happen. Glad I was here today," Bud Donovan says as he shakes Grandpa's hand. "We're all lucky, aren't we, boys?" He finishes by looking directly at Slater now.

Before the manager walks away, Grandpa has Slater slide over to the passenger seat before he pulls forward into the parking space again.

"Are we still going fishing, Grandpa?" Slater asks slowly.

Graham's eyes bore into Slater from the backseat because Graham knows if fishing gets cancelled, this won't be the first time something gets ruined because of what Slater has done.

"Son, let's just think about this for a minute. What happened here today is very serious." Grandpa turns his right shoulder to speak to Slater face-to-face. "Can you tell me how many things could have gone wrong just now?"

"I already said I was sorry," Slater says curtly, feeling like this is going to be a lecture from the person he least expected to ever hear one from.

"Slater, now, son, I want a direct answer. Let's think this through. How many different things could have gone wrong here today?"

"Well, we could have hit a car," Slater starts thoughtfully, "and maybe if a slow person was walking behind us, we could have run them over," he says, satisfied that this should be enough for Grandpa.

"What else could have happened?"

"I don't know," Slater says, looking at his knuckles.

"What if that minivan wasn't there to be hit, what if no car was there to block you, where would you have rolled to then?"

"I don't know," Slater says, more defiantly this time.

"Son, look behind you. What do you see?"

Graham turns his head real fast behind him to see the busy street of traffic at an intersection with lights and lots of cars.

"Ooooh, Slater, we would have been mushed in traffic," Graham says so obviously.

"I see it," Slater says dejectedly. "I said I was sorry. I just didn't think that the gears were so easy to slip." He bows his head to stare at his bare knuckles once again.

"Son, I don't care about the damage to this old car. I care about the safety of you and Graham," Grandpa says as he reaches a gentle finger under Slater's chin to prop him up so Grandpa can see his eyes. "Nothing would make my heart ache more than if something happened to one of you, especially on my watch," he says mightily before his eyes tear up. Wiping them with both of his hands, he finishes, "I'd never be able to forgive myself, son."

"Oh, Grandpa, I'm real sorry," Slater says, moving in quickly to hug Grandpa, hiding his own tears with his hair now grown long over his eyes, "real sorry."

"Okay, ladies, are we going fishing or not?" Graham says, hoping the trip is still on.

"Well, I have half a mind to take you straight home, but seeing as how I think you just learned a pretty important lesson, let's go to the pond anyway even though it's getting to be so late. I hope there are still some fish that'll be bitin'," Grandpa says with a warm smile.

Even though there were no fish hooked from the pond this day, the hours that Graham and Slater spent with their Grandpa were the best part of this afternoon. Grandpa told stories again about his days in the war and the kinds of meals he got to eat that came out of a can or powdered foods that only required you to add a bit of water.

When there was nothing left to share about his life, he made up stories about little island natives who tried to play jokes on the sleeping giant. Graham would giggle and giggle and beg Grandpa to tell another. Slater would laugh heartily at the really funny parts and then tell Grandpa all about his own stories, like the Halloween Haunt.

Before the day would end, Grandpa and Slater and Graham would stop by the store on their way home—a different grocery this time—to buy three of the biggest trout there were. They'd take it in the car and unwrap the fish so each of them could practice stringing a trout on the hook to show their mom what they caught today. Some years they were able to have much better luck, but it never mattered much to Lynn—she knew that trout only ran in streams. She was perfectly content to know her boys were so happy to be in cahoots with their grandpa.

This made for two secrets that Lynn Hannigan never found out about that day.

CHAPTER 11

Thanksgiving Pie Surprise

With two days to go before the pie fund-raiser, Slater has it worked out in his head that he and Macaroni and Phil only need thirty-one more dollars if they each want to take home the pies the student council promised them.

"I say we ask each kid in the class to chip in one measly dollar," Macaroni says logically.

"But, will they all, really?" Phil says, speculating that some of the girls probably won't even want to go in on it.

"Well, what if we hide something from each of them that they really want back and pretend to write a ransom note and then we get paid the reward for finding it," Slater says, thinking this could be a genius way of making extra money.

"But, won't it be kinda obvious when none of *our* stuff goes missing?" Macaroni points out helpfully.

"Well, what if we just take one of the girls' notebooks. You know they write all their perfect notes in there. They would probably pay like a hundred dollars to get that stuff back," Slater says, still trying to keep hope alive that this might be the answer.

"I don't know," Phil says, mulling it over slowly. "Whose notebook? Not Kerry Ko's. Dude, she kind of scares me."

"No, no, not Kerry Ko's—she'd be so mad she'd get revenge on us for sure," Slater says laughing but in a nervous way. "What about Sibley's? And what if we took her fancy pencil case, too? She loves that thing." Slater finishes with his grand idea.

"I don't know, man, we could get in a lot of trouble if we get caught," Macaroni says worriedly.

"Principal Daly would go ballistic on us, and I just got to this school. I don't want my mom to yank me out and send me to a new school all over again," Phil says, fearing the worst.

"You guys, I was just kidding about the ransom anyway," Slater says, laughing. "But what if her stuff just *happened* to go missing and we *happened* to be the ones to find it? Don't you think she'd be grateful enough to give us a reward?" Slater wonders.

"Actually, Sibley would be the type to decorate Wanted signs and put them all over the school for her missing notebook and art pencils," Macaroni says, imagining Sibley out of her mind with worry about how she would ever pass a test without her notes to study.

"But how do we do it? When is she ever not near her stuff?" Phil asks innocently.

"We need to create a distraction, something that gets the whole class's attention, and then just reach inside her desk and grab them," Slater says powerfully.

"What's the distraction gonna be? You're not thinking about pulling a fire alarm?—no way can we even get away with that," Macaroni says, terrified this might be Slater's way out.

"No, I wasn't thinking fire alarm, even I'm not *that* stupid," Slater says convincingly. "I was thinking, like, one of you brings a spider into the room and then points it out when you see it there on the floor," Slater says happily about his plan.

"Yeah, you know how the girls will all start screaming about a spider," Macaroni says, laughing.

"And the guys will want to come over and see it for themselves," Phil says assuredly.

"Right, so that gets everyone out of their seats, and then Miss Burbank will be trying to get everyone calm, so she'll probably put the spider on a napkin and then just take it outside," Slater says, imagining his plan will come off without a hitch.

"But, how long do we wait before Sibley is supposed to write Wanted signs? We only have two days before the deadline," Macaroni says anxiously.

"Well, we could give her, like, some suggestions that maybe she should put up some posters about her lost stuff, then everyone at school would be on the lookout," Slater proposes.

"Ooh, and then we could add in, real casual like, maybe her stuff would be replaced faster if the first person to find it gets, like, a little reward," Phil says brightly.

"The thing is, you can't even act all suspicious. You gotta not even be looking at Sibley when she starts going through her things to find her pencils, 'cause as soon as she does, you know she's gonna look at *me*," Slater says real seriously.

"Yeah, she'll probably even accuse you before she even finishes looking in her backpack," Macaroni agrees, nodding his head vigorously.

"You gotta just play it real cool or you're gonna blow the whole thing and then we get zero pie."

Slater has laid out the game plan, and both Macaroni and Phil know what they are supposed to do. While Phil goes looking for spiders, trying to determine which could be the biggest one to draw attention, Macaroni starts paying really close attention to all of Sibley's habits. He knows which color pencil she uses to do spelling work and which one she uses to take notes about social studies. Whenever we are learning a different subject, she pulls out one of her colored highlighters to draw a bubble around today's date in her notebook, and then begins writing in a pencil that matches both her highlighter *and* her stretchy vinyl book cover. The plan is to find the spider during lunch and then the whole Sibley Spider episode can begin.

What the boys do not see coming is the heartless tactic of Miss Burbank. She squashes their plan when she squashes that spider as soon as she sees it crawling from three rows away.

"How did she even know it was there?" Macaroni asks, completely flummoxed.

"Dude, I don't know. I thought that was a pretty good spider. It was all thick and black and moved pretty good, too," Slater says with pride about Phil's spider picking.

"What do we do now?" Phil asks the guys.

"Okay, we've got three of us and three pies. We can sell forks for $1 to every kid in the class who wants one. For every fork, they get one bite of a pie. One of you is gonna have to give up your pie and we'll all share the other two," Slater says, as if he has the final word.

"Wait a minute, why should I have to give up *my* pie? Pumpkin is my favorite," Macaroni says with his arms crossed over his chest and tummy.

"Come on, Slater, there's got to be another way. I agree with Macaroni, I don't want to give up my pie either, especially since we picked up all that trash in the park with your Gramps," Phil says democratically.

"Oh, I'll remember this. Fine, then," Slater says in a huff. "I'll give up mine, so long as we all split *your* pies equally. I don't want to be gypped," he says firmly.

With a new plan in place to sell the other thirty-one classmates a fork for their own personal bite of pie, Slater and his friends wait to see what tomorrow brings—hoping this time their plan will not backfire.

The next day at Esther Bookman Elementary, there is a buzz in the air as Slater, Phil, and Macaroni begin their fork campaign.

While students are lined up waiting for Miss Burbank, the boys have started whispering to their peers the many ways they can get in on the pie action because there is certainly going to be enough to share with all of the money they have raised.

Macaroni gets so carried away persuading everybody that he tells them they will all be able to enjoy two inches of whipped cream on top of that forkful of pie. What he does not know is that Phil is doing the same thing to entice his classmates in line to give up a dollar by telling them that there will *also* be Oreo crumb topping to scoop onto your fork.

Slater is the only one who sells the $1 fork for just what it was supposed to be, a bite of pie—however, he does promise the *first* ten bites to his *first* ten donors by convincing them that there might not be as big of a bite left for the *last* ten forks. Clever boy.

With the money promised to be in hand the next day, Slater feels confident that he can announce their super big collection when student council comes around this morning to remind every class about tomorrow's deadline.

"All right, everybody," Miss Burbank says, trying to get her class's attention, "you have one day to review before the test tomorrow. I want to remind you that this will be the last score I enter into the gradebook before report cards are due." She eyes each of her rows.

"Some of you have worked very hard these past few months and you are off to a very good start," she says. These students immediately sit up straighter in their chairs knowing she must be speaking about *each* of them. "And there are others of you in here who I still expect will deliver the great things that I know you can accomplish if you sharpen your focus." These last words are lost on the children who should be paying attention.

"We have practiced this before, so on the count of three, you have six minutes to write your test question on the two index cards on top of your desk. Remember, only two questions per person about the category that your group has been assigned to research. Do you need clarification?" Miss Burbank asks, looking around until she is satisfied. "Okay, timer is set for six minutes. Go!" she says enthusiastically, dinging her bellman's bell atop her desk.

Clusters of furniture shift quickly away from row formation. Backpacks are caught in the scramble with their straps stuck under metal legs that now wobble on their uneven foundation. The children are eager to stump their friends. After all, the group that comes up with the most challenging questions expected to be on the test will receive high praise from friends who never would have thought otherwise to study for *that* one. Plus, Miss Burbank will write some kind of excellent comment on the report card about your leadership abilities. Who doesn't want that?

"Slater, we only have three minutes left," Sibley White says sharply as she sees that nothing is on either of his cards yet.

"I know, Sibley—I learned how to tell time in second grade," he snaps back.

"Second grade? Wow, I learned it before I went into kindergarten," Sibley says sympathetically, as if poor Slater has some obvious deficiencies. "I hope you are going to find some math problems to make our group look good, Slater—there aren't any about clocks on your pages," Sibley says in a spiteful tone, keeping her head down and her pencil moving.

Slater grumbles to himself something that Sibley cannot hear. Sometimes he would just like to take all of her books and throw them into the boys' bathroom and see how smart she would be then.

"Final minute, class. How many groups have one question already done for each person?" Miss Burbank asks with an encouraging voice.

All groups raise their hands except for Slater's.

"Does any group need more time?"

Looking around the room for the thumbs-up signal from each group captain, she feels compelled to check in with Sibley. "Are you needing any more time over here?"

"I think we're good, Miss Burbank," Sibley says hesitantly while she watches Slater feverishly scratch out the first card and start over again.

"Okay," Miss Burbank says with her usual tone of cautious optimism. "Final minute, everybody. Make sure each person has two questions ready to go."

Slater is onto his second card, which is still blank while he flips through the section of his textbook about algebra.

"All right, here's your final count. Five, four," Miss Burbank says slowly as Slater starts scribbling as fast as he can, "three, two," she strings out the syllables for as long as she can, watching him work, "one. Time's up, guys."

Slater slams down the pencil with the look of victory on his face and says to Sibley White, "Ha! Bet you couldn't even solve this last one."

As soon as she is tempted to give him a snarling reply, she thinks better of it since Miss Burbank is looking her way, probably more so to see if *both* of Slater's cards are filled out.

"Group 1, I'd like you to get up and go stand with your backs against our library wall in a straight line facing the other side of the room." When she is sure that they each have their two cards and are standing correctly, she moves on. "Group 3, you should be standing up here with me, facing the back of the room," she directs simply. However after two of the kids face off against one another, she has to intervene. "No, not playing against your own team members. *All* of you turn to face the back of the room. Yes, that's better.

"Group 5, stand with your backs against our window ledge. Good job, Group 5; that was fast."

Miss Burbank finishes sorting the rest of her class to play stump the student. As they begin their first challenge round, student council pops in with the final reminder before tomorrow's collection for the Thanksgiving Pie Challenge.

"Hi, girls," Miss Burbank greets Charity Bronstein and Gina Gomez. "Can you make it kind of quick? We're right in the middle of a test review," she asks sweetly.

"Sure, Miss Burbank. Sorry about the interruption. As you know,

I'm Charity, and this is Gina and—" Charity is completely cut off by Miss Burbank, who is beyond acting polite about this disruption.

"Girls, you have ten seconds."

"Um, sorry, are you guys going to have your $100 ready for tomorrow?" Charity clumsily asks. She had a fun little reminder speech, but this kind of pressure makes her forget everything she had planned.

"Remember? For the pie challenge so Miss Burbank can take home a pie after you throw a whipped cream pie in her face?" Gina tries to fill in equally awkwardly.

"I don't think my class will be participating this year, girls. Thanks for dropping by," Miss Burbank readily dismisses them, and as they thank her for her time and apologize again, a voice sounds from the other side of the room.

"Miss Burbank," Macaroni calls out, politely waving his hand.

"Yes, Joe, do you have a contribution you would like to make to student council?"

"Actually, Slater does," he says slyly and throws both of his hands to Slater as if to welcome him to his invisible stage.

"Hey, Charity, we have our money and we'll give it to you tomorrow, okay?" Slater says with a Cheshire cat half smile.

Oh, she can feel it. The hairs on the back of her neck stand up. Miss Burbank rubs her palm along the backside of her pearl necklace, thinking that maybe the fastener has come undone. But no, she feels a tightening in her shoulders that is always the first sign of something going terribly wrong.

"Great, Room 14 has earned $100 to pie their teacher. Miss Burbank, will you be accepting the challenge, or will you be paying to forfeit?" Miss Burbank feels completely put on the spot. She did not think it would get to this point at all. She never heard any scuttlebutt about raising money and assumed her class was not taking the challenge seriously.

"I guess I accept the challenge, and I will pick the person who raises the most money to pie me—gently, of course," she says, trying to throw a convincing smile to her students.

"Actually, Charity, we don't have a hundred dollars—" Slater starts before Charity jumps in.

"I thought you just said you did, Slater—" Charity is the one cut off this time.

"We got $300! And you made a promise that we would get three pies, something special you said you could arrange, right?" Slater says, winking at his friends while the whole class erupts in a spontaneous cheer.

Miss Burbank is completely flabbergasted by this news. As she sits at the front of the room in her director's chair—reserved for special conferences she has with her children when they visit with her at her desk—she is wondering if this is going to mean what she thinks it means.

"Wow! You did it? That is amazing, Slater! Your class is to be congratulated, and you know what this means—" Charity speaks quickly to get to the good part before Gina steals her thunder.

"You get to pie Miss Burbank *three* times!" There, Gina beat her to it.

Oh, no! Exactly what I suspected. The thoughts ramble around in Miss Burbank's brain as to how she can get out of this predicament without looking like a poor sport.

"But, Miss Burbank, we can only give you just the one pie to take home," Charity says, turning toward Miss Burbank with a half-smile before she returns to face the class with her full-on grin. "We're so excited! If you guys actually have all of that money tomorrow, you will be the top winners of the whole school!"

The class cheers again, and friends high-five each other. Nobody could have predicted that a class full of ten-year-olds could be this excited about a forkful of pie, whipped cream, and Oreo crumble topping. In actuality, it's not the fork that they are celebrating. It is the fact that they won. They beat the whole school, and now they have bragging rights as the coolest fifth-grade class to leave Esther Bookman Elementary behind next year when they go to middle school.

This feeling of victory lasts for one whole day.

"Okay, class, you've had quite a good bit of news, but now we need to settle back into our teams to begin our review," Miss Burbank says loudly, tapping her bell multiple times and also using her quiet hand signal, hoping that at least half of the class will follow her lead.

Finally, there is a hush in the room, even though the energy feels electrifying.

"Let's get back to the job you have prepared—ready, set, go!"

Immediately, the noise level returns to the room, but this time it feels different. All of the assigned A teams quiz the opposing B teams with their two index questions first, and then the B teams throw out their own challenges to the A teams. Miss Burbank walks the room to listen intently for any student who has anticipated tomorrow's test questions accurately. Yes, this has happened in the past and it is always so thrilling. Usually, she can tell which children are most likely to think like a teacher, but sometimes there is a surprise or two from her students.

Today is no different. Slowly, she meanders to Sibley's group. She does not want Slater to feel that he is the target of her "picking on him," as he likes to say, but she is genuinely interested in what questions he has carved out to stump his fellow students.

"Vern has 9 mechanical pencils at the beginning of the school year. Roxanne has p fewer pencils than Vern. Choose the expression that shows how many pencils Roxanne has. A) $9 - p$, B) 9, C) $9 + p$, D) $p + 9$." Slater is so proud of his question because most of the students in Team B have to read it twice before they can answer. So far, he has stumped two kids because "A) $9 - p$" is the right answer.

Miss Burbank likes what she sees. Slater is fully engaged and has a good first question. She moves swiftly around the room to check that each of the other teams has made it through the second round of questions before she taps the bell signaling Groups 2, 4, and 6 to rotate clockwise, which she has to choreograph carefully because not everyone moves in the same direction. *Digital clocks have really ruined that expression.*

While the students are still enjoying another lightning round of stumping their new opposing teams, Miss Burbank sneaks behind Slater in time to hear his second question.

"I am filling a big washtub to give my dog a bath, and I need to use two other smaller containers that each have the capacity of 0.2L. If each of these smaller containers has been filled 6 times and then poured into the washtub, how much water (in milliliters) is in the washtub?

A) 120ml, B) 240ml, C) 2400ml, D)1200ml."

"This is a very good question, Slater. In fact, it is on the test tomorrow; good for you," Miss Burbank says brightly. "Tobey, do you know the answer yet?"

Tobey thinks and thinks, screwing up his face and furrowing his eyebrows as he keeps staring at the answers. "I don't know, is it B) 240ml?"

"Well, Slater, is that the answer?" Miss Burbank allows Slater to play teacher here.

"No, dude, you got close, but it's C) 2400ml because you gotta multiply it all out," Slater says, telling Tobey he'll show him where it is in the book so Tobey knows what part to study better tonight.

Tobey is wondering why he needs to study anyway since now he already knows the answer for at least one of the test questions.

"Okay, everybody, how'd we do? Who got stumped by at least one question?" Miss Burbank asks as twenty hands shoot into the air. "How about stumped on two to five questions?" Again, she sees hands in the air from the same people. "What about six to ten questions missed?" Only about ten hands remain in the air this time. "Do I dare to ask who missed most of the questions from today?" With lots of giggles, only four hands remain proudly in the air. "Okay, you know what we always say about failing, right?"

"Yep, you can only go up from here," Janice from the back of the room says with a big grin.

"I heard a lot of really good material covered today, so if you are still feeling like you are on shaky ground, now you know what you need to study, right?" Miss Burbank says to a room full of nodding heads. "Pull out your study guides and place them on top of your desk for us to finish filling out after lunch. As soon as I see you back in rows and you've got your paper on your desk, I will dismiss you."

With the scurrying of furniture being pushed into crooked rows and some lunch bags being mushed beneath thoughtless feet, Miss Burbank says good-bye to Slater's row first, then Sibley's, then the others as they straighten themselves out. "See you after lunch, everybody; have a good one," Miss Burbank calls after them.

✐ ✐ ✐ ✐

"Well, Dana, what are you going to do? *Three* pies? Whoever thought this was going to happen?" Janet from first grade asks, completely aghast. It is exactly what the other teachers have been thinking, too, ever since student council made the rounds this morning, announcing how competitive Room 14 was with assurances they have raised *triple* the amount needed for the pie challenge.

"I can tell you this—Slater will *not* be throwing any pie in my face. I think I have it figured out, but I will let you know." With this sly comment, it is obvious Miss Burbank no longer wishes to discuss the subject. Her only parting statement is, "That boy sure knows math."

✐   ✐   ✐   ✐

When Room 14 lines up the next day, high with anticipation about taking their test in the morning and then seeing Slater throw pies at their teacher, imagine their surprise when at precisely 8:03 a.m., they are aroused from their chatter by the sound of a strong, throaty whistle, followed by a firm bellow that is not the sound of Miss Burbank.

"Attention! Students, face the front. I am going to number you off today, and this is what you will be called until I learn your name. I recognize some family names on the roster from when I taught your older siblings—or maybe even your parents. You, Number 14. Do I see your mouth moving while I am speaking?"

A neck snap to the center of the line from the other students ahead of and behind Sibley causes her to turn three shades of red from all of the unwanted attention.

"I'm—I'm sorry, I was just telling someone to stop pushing me," Sibley says with a slight crack in her voice.

"Number 15—take three steps back. Number 13—do the same going forward. Good. Now everyone else, I'll say this one time only this morning—*everyone* move three steps away from the person next to you. There will be no pushing, no touching, no chatting, no patting, no whining, no sneering, no cheering, or anything else to communicate within the line. Are we clear?"

"Yes, yes, yeah," comes the feeble and disorganized response from the class.

"I said, are we clear? When I ask you a direct question, you are to respond to me in unison—precisely, and strongly, with your best posture and forward attention, locking eyes with mine. This way I know we are both communicating. Straighten up, troops. Look alive. Forward heads. Now, for the last time, are we clear?"

"Yes, sir," comes the only natural reply from this class who looks fully regimented like any other military unit. This substitute has put the fear into them all right, the likes of which they have never experienced before. And while they have never been formally introduced—they have heard the rumors, plenty of rumors.

These kids have considered themselves so lucky that she retired before they could ever be in her class. The horror stories their families recount about the best and worst teacher *they* ever had at Esther Bookman Elementary always results in the same name.

Ms. Elsa Wilson corrects Miss Burbank's students on the right way to address her by quietly hissing, "Yes, sir, *madame*."

CHAPTER 12

Meet Madame Wilson

If only one could have read the *internal* expressions of the students standing in Miss Burbank's line, they would have matched the same look of shock streaking across all of their faces now—crooked mouths fully open and eyes popping out of their heads, sheer and utter screams of terror confined inside voice boxes frozen with fear in the back of their throats.

Not Mrs. Wilson, the singular thought they all share fills their little minds.

"Number 1, bring your entire line silently inside. As soon as you have found your places, you are to clear your desks, pull out three of your best pencils and erasers, and zip your backpacks completely closed. Do we understand one another?"

"Yes, sir, madame," they recite as they have been trained.

"Very good now. You have exactly the time it takes for me to count to five to do as you have been told. I do not feel the need to express what will happen if I must go as far as to count to number *six*," she says suspiciously, looking through the rows until each child feels an invisible laser imprint across their foreheads from her penetrating glare. "Do I?" she asks, dragging out the final syllable for much longer than it needs to be carried.

"Yes, sir—I mean no, sir, madame." The kids are so taken off guard by this new routine that they have no idea what they are supposed to be saying yes and no to.

"That would be no, sir, madame," she says with a chill in her voice.

"Yes, sir, madame—we meant no, sir, madame," Sibley says on behalf of the class. She is the only one who can figure out what is going on and one of the only few who is brave enough to call any attention to herself.

"One," she begins seriously. The kids had no idea she would begin this fast, and they scramble, desperate to remember what she wanted them to get out of their backpacks. Everyone watches Sibley White and Kerry Ko set up their own desks and follows suit quickly. "Two, thu-ree," she counts, putting dramatic emphasis on the word *three* by splitting it into two syllables, as if she has been a well-trained opera singer rolling her r's. The deepness of her voice is completely different than the light, sing-song voice of Miss Burbank.

Slater cannot find three pencils even though he knows they are in his backpack somewhere. Desperate to not look unprepared, he whispers to Sibley in front of him, "Can I borrow a pencil?"

Sibley knew it was coming. It happens every test. So she drops the loaner pencil at her feet for Slater to easily pick up once she kicks it a little farther back his direction. She is still grateful he made her group look good yesterday with his math prep questions, and he gets so few rewards, the least she can do is slide him one of her uglier pencils. If he can stand to look at its zebra pattern in stripes of tangerine and lime green, this one has the perfect number lead needed for test taking. Maybe it will even bring him a little luck today.

"Young man, what is it you need?" Elsa Wilson spies him awkwardly reaching outside of his personal perimeter and wonders what business he could have ankle side of the young lady in front of him.

"Oh, ma'am, sir-madame," Slater begins, quite confused as to what title he should use in this instance, "umm, I just dropped my pencil here and I was trying to pick it up real quietly. Sorry, sir-madame."

Elsa Wilson does not even mind that he has fumbled with her name—or told a lie in the process. Clearly, that uniquely gorgeous pencil belongs to the girl in front who has neatly laid out three others just like it in the same striped pattern with different color hues obviously from the same gift set. *I will watch this boy closely during the test*, she thinks.

"Carry on, then," she says while he finger crawls his way back to his desk from the floor. "Class, now that you look prepared for your morning test, I will be inspecting your rows to be certain that your backpacks are zipped completely. I do not wish to see loose papers peeking out—especially not your study guide accidentally sitting there all by its lonesome."

She continues, "Be sure your packs are tight beneath your seat. That square between the four legs of your desk is your personal space perimeter, and you should organize more efficiently if you are struggling to get your load to fit within it. Just like the airlines, anyone whose bag cannot be stowed underneath the seat beneath you, please raise your hand so I can dismiss you to drop it along the wall outside of our classroom. Just like the airlines, I am sure it will be safe there," she says, offering a wicked little laugh.

Everyone looks around, wondering if she is for real. Some kids wrestle with the girth of their bags but will keep shoving to make it fit because they know it won't be sitting outside when the bell rings. Someone will find their backpack all by itself, rip it apart like a savage, and then throw the emptied canvas into the cafeteria, saving the good lunch and the calculator for themselves.

Madame Wilson plunks her heavy metal cane onto the floor with the downbeat of every step of her left foot. She is not going to risk a broken hip in a messy classroom. She also does not need to worry about coming into contact with a sticky child when her cane works like an extended finger. She can point to the mess on top of a desk where a trail from pink eraser mark crumbs appears, dark and ant-like. She can tap upon the floor in just the spot where the child has lazily discarded pencil shavings from a personal sharpener—naughty, naughty.

The cane will not stop its erratic tapping until a tissue has been retrieved and all shavings gently placed into it. For the child who sheds tears of remorse, she will take the greatest pity—providing a wide swath of sticky tape to more easily remove the collection of debris upon the floor in one fell swoop.

Room 14 has a sense of urgency that has not been felt this year. The kids look different to each other now. They are perspiring and red-faced, downtrodden in fact. They finally appear to be the closest version of professional-looking students Mr. Daly has ever seen, and when he walks through the door to welcome back Elsa Wilson, he marvels at what a remarkable group of children we have here.

It's like he has never seen them before. Does he even remember the last time he was in Room 14 when pencils dangled from the ceiling? "My, Mrs. Wilson, it is good to see you back at Esther Bookman. I heard you were substituting today, and I wanted to personally thank you for your service and remind our students of the behavior expectations we have for our Badgers when we have guests on campus," Principal Daly says charmingly, shaking her hand vigorously while eyeing all of the pupils. "I must say, children, to see you sitting so tall and still in your chairs with your room looking so tidy, you look quite impressive. Obviously, you are all making your acquaintance today, and I expect you shall get along just fine," Principal Daly says smiling from ear to ear and thinking, *What could be the matter that Dana Burbank complains so?*

"Before we get to our morning test, I want to properly greet you today. Good morning, class," Elsa Wilson says mightily, though without a smile. "Class, it is expected that you will in turn greet me in the same manner; and since a greeting is less formal than a reply to a direct order, you may call me Madame Wilson, which I prefer."

Collectively the class follows her lead. "Good Morning, Madame Wilson," they say brightly in unison.

"Oh, you have a lovely quality to your voice. It sounds so melodious, thank you," she says, perching her reading glasses upon the bridge of her nose, suspended from a personal chain connected to both arms so they can swing from her neck until needed again.

"As some of you may be new to this school and do not know me, I have been a teacher at Esther Bookman Elementary for forty years. In fact, I have watched many of these buildings be erected as our school needs have grown in the past twenty-five years. I have taught many parents who have also sent their children through my class, so do not be surprised to learn when you go home that your mother or father was one of my favorite students—perhaps.

"According to your substitute plans for today, your teacher Miss Burbank has written a note apologizing to you for not being well enough to stay for your test, but says that she trusts you are well-prepared with the material and she wishes you all the best of luck. She also wants you to remember that the usual rules apply during testing environments—no getting up from your seat for any reason, no talking to a neighbor, and no using a calculator, and remember to show your work.

"I also have a few rules that I have found to be helpful to my students in the past years to lessen their anxiety on test days. Simply do not ask me to come to your desk for the purpose of collecting your test ahead of the hour you have to finish. There is no prize for being done first, and I often find those students of mine who rush through the process often make sloppy mistakes that cost them precious points.

"Finally, I require absolute silence. You may doodle on the scratch paper I will be providing you if there is still time left, but you are in no way to be signaling to your friends that you have finished. In fact, I travel with thirty privacy folders in the event that a teacher does not have a classroom set in supply. Do you use these for tests?"

"No, but I would like a privacy folder, Madame Wilson," Kerry Ko says graciously.

"So would I, please, ma'am," says Sibley, equally grateful. Both of these girls know that they are always forced to use the whole of their arm and sometimes their long hair to cover their answers from wandering eyes seated near them.

"Wonderful, girls. When you tell me your names after school, I will write a positive note to your teacher about your enthusiasm," Madame Wilson says cheerfully. "But don't fret, class, I have enough folders to go around.

"There is a second remark here, something about your Thanksgiving Pie Challenge. Miss Burbank sends her regrets that she will miss out on all of the excitement and simply asks that if there is a volunteer from class who would like to take her place, then Slater may throw the pies at that spirited person." Madame Wilson only finishes reading partway before she is distracted by rustling in the room of murmurs and sidebars. "Class, do not be confused, I have not quite finished reading your instructions, but I can tell this has stirred you. I feel this will be better resolved once we have finished our testing for the morning. I trust you can find your focus to maintain a proper testing environment, yes?" she says clearly and seriously.

"Yes, sir, madame," the entire class sings. They are certainly catching on now.

She stands at the front of the class with blank paper in her hand and pinches enough for each person at the head of each row to pass behind them one sheet for each person. Satisfied that all backpacks have been tucked away and that all students look prepared, she then distributes the privacy folders. These are to stand tall to protect the answers each student has supplied from his or her own brain.

All Macaroni can do is to sigh and shrug. He looks across the aisle to Slater two rows away as if to say, "I don't know, how am I gonna do this test?"

Usually Macaroni and Slater have some kind of system worked out to give each other a little support just to point a guy in the right direction. It's not actual cheating if you don't get caught—at least that's *their* theory.

For the first time, Slater has little to say. Something about Elsa Wilson has him scared. Slater can only purse his lips to the side, hoping this sly gesture will be enough to provide reassurance to Macaroni that he himself is no better off.

Once the class confirms that they are clear about all of the testing rules, and once Elsa Wilson has passed out each testing booklet with the strictest instruction to not begin until the entire class has received their answer document, silence takes over.

Usually during tests, Miss Burbank will work away at her desk. Not Madame Wilson. Today, she stands at attention in front of the class, first smoothing out her long wool plaid skirt that she bought on her travels to Ireland. She unbuttons only the bottom three holes of the double thick fisherman's knit cardigan she is wearing before she takes a seat on the director's chair reserved for student conferences. She sees to it that the bow from her blouse is still precisely tied at her neck and that the tails of the wide ribbon are not uneven in their lengths. She manages to keep her cane hooked to her elbow while taking care to position herself upon this most uncomfortable wooden seat.

She pulls from her upright suitcase on wheels a tapestry bag no bigger than the size of a bowling ball. From its contents, she withdraws a skein of turquoise yarn along with two long knitting needles at one end of a scarf that looks nearly finished. This is a habit she has obviously mastered because Madame Wilson's fingers never stop moving, though her gaze never leaves the room where she watches her testers like a hawk.

Nearly forty-five minutes into the examination, some students are clearly finishing ahead of the others. She will commend them later for staying so intently noiseless. Instead of doodling, they are each transfixed by the gentle clacking of sharp metal needles tapping each other for an instant as she continues knitting the scarf that has grown down her legs and begun to bunch upon the floor in the same way toilet paper does when the dispenser makes up its mind to unravel all by itself.

If she were typing, she could not be any faster. A dinger would be ringing every sixty seconds when the return carriage would sound. As more students finish, thankful to not feel rushed, they too become mesmerized. Her freckled hands work so speedily. Would *their* grandmothers be able to magically knit a scarf so fast? They wonder.

Kerry Ko sketches a portrait of Madame Wilson sitting on a throne, with a long cape ascending in front of her with the yarn and needles attached to her hands.

Once everyone is finished with the test, and Madame Wilson has collected all of the materials, the kids are free to let out a huge sigh of relief that this portion of the day is over.

"Children, you have behaved yourselves very well this morning. I must commend you thus far, and I will be sure that your teacher, Miss Burbank, hears this bit of good news. I expect nothing less from you as the day ensues," Madame Wilson says in her operatic voice. "The next part of your lesson plan is to work on your science project with your partner. This seems like a good time to take a much-needed stretch break first. Everybody up. That's right, get up and out of your seats, chop, chop," Madame Wilson says, clapping her hands together in a staccato beat.

"Make yourselves tall, tall trees and stretch toward the sun." Madame Wilson has gotten the boys to perform her ridiculous poses for the better part of ten minutes. Never would any other teacher on this campus believe that Slater and his brood were doing yoga poses with Madame Wilson. "My goodness I feel better, don't you, too?"

"Yes, sir, madame," the class says, rather enjoying their delight in this new and unusual salute.

"This seems like the right time to ask you about your special pie day. Who can tell me about your plans?" Madame Wilson asks curiously.

"Well, that should be Slater, since he helped to raise the most money for our school fund-raiser," Kerry Ko states generously.

"Who is Slater? Raise your hand. Is it you, Number 12?" Madame Wilson asks in Slater's general direction, reminding them that she still only knows them by line number positions.

"Yeah, that's me, um, sir-madame," Slater says, clearing his throat. "The deal is we get to pie our teacher, but our teacher isn't here, and I guess she says we can pie each other, so I want to pie Macaroni," Slater says, laughing and looking over at Macaroni who buries his head as if to say, *No way, man, I knew it.* "And then I want to also pie Phil," Slater continues, pointing to Phil, who has the same reaction but is quick to make claims on the third pie.

"And then, Madame Wilson, I would love to throw the third pie at Slater," Phil says, pointing at Slater and looking around the room to rile up the class who all cheer him on by saying, "Slater, Slater, Slater!"

"Well, my goodness, it looks as if you have things pretty well planned out. Are there any objections here?" Madame Wilson asks politely, but no one makes any motions to the contrary, so it looks like Slater and his friends get their wishes granted.

"Then I will submit your names to the student council representatives at recess today, and we will all look forward to seeing you get whipped cream all over your faces at lunch. Have proper provisions been made for the cleanup process? Certainly we do not wish to resume our afternoon schedule with sticky messes and dirty faces." Only Elsa Wilson could get away with sounding like she is a wicked character from a Disney movie. She is obviously so ancient that kids have to give her some respect. Also, who would ever want to defy her, especially if she had been your parent's teacher, too?

So far, Madame Wilson and Room 14 are getting along just fine. In fact they should be old friends—after all, this was indeed Mrs. Wilson's room. She is amazed by all the beautiful changes their teacher Miss Burbank has made to the walls and the cheerful learning centers she has established. Still, there might be a thing or two Elsa Wilson could still teach these students if she were to come back to Esther Bookman Elementary. Her retirement is not quite what she expected. After spending the past five months traveling, what else is left for her to do?

Miss Burbank got her wish to not be pied by Slater Hannigan. She found a way to leave her class and let the students have their fun. And fun is what they have indeed with Elsa Wilson cheering them on loudly, wildly waving her cane in the air with snarling screams of, "Get him, young man" as she tries to act out parts of jousting competitions with her cane.

The students in Room 14 go off to their holidays with families who do indeed remember their time in Mrs. Wilson's class. Some, though, have quite delicious stories to tell about the time their friends suffered consequences nearly unrepeatable that are met with insistent pleas of *Tell us, tell us* from their children.

The hours pass with each parent recalling stories from what they *personally* witnessed when Mrs. Wilson would do unannounced desk inspections by first toppling the furniture to the ground for all of its contents to spill across the floor. Oh yes, there were many rules in Mrs. Wilson's class, none less important than the first: *Every child must leave with the education intended for the day.*

CHAPTER 13

Slater's Big Reward

Dear Dana,

I am so sorry you missed seeing your students in action today. They were all quite brilliantly behaved, and I got to know a few who must be among your star pupils. Sibley and Kerry were quite eager to take precautionary measures to keep their exams hidden when I offered privacy carousels to the whole class using the folders I keep on hand—these really ought to benefit every teacher who invests in a class set. Slater was particularly helpful today in organizing the plan for who would be receiving whipped cream pies in the face (Phil and a boy called Macaroni—that can't be his real name, is it, dear?). Oh, it was such fun to witness. I hope you find the room to be orderly—each of the children picked up twenty items of lint off the floor as their ticket out the door. As usual, it does my heart good to be back in Room 14. Perhaps I can help out again, dear. Retirement is for the birds.

Most heartfelt regards,
Elsa

Miss Burbank is happy to read that there were no disciplinary issues in her absence. *Perhaps the class is maturing*, she muses. The note is placed neatly on the stack of tests that were collected before the Thanksgiving break. Miss Burbank is back from the holiday a little earlier this morning in the event her room needs tidying before the students return from vacation.

Thankfully, she now has time instead to grade the tests sitting in front of her. The answer documents are in an electronic scan format that will take all of ten minutes for the results to be read by the machine. For every problem marked incorrect, the Scantron makes a hammer sound. The first time she used this machine years ago, she was not sure which direction the Scantron was supposed to face—only when it sounded like the rat-a-tat-tat of machine gun rivets did another teacher rush over to explain that the answer key was in upside down.

In order to be sure the machine is working and the answer key is correct, Miss Burbank has learned to first scan the test from the student who will most likely perform the best to make sure there are no processing errors. She runs Kerry Ko's right away.

The sound of two hammers means Kerry has only missed two problems. The machine seems to be working just fine.

Miss Burbank scans Sibley's next, then Neimer's, both of which come out as she expected with less than five bullets between them. She runs the rest, quickly pushing through each paper strip, waiting for it to spit out the other end. Like a log going into the woodchopper, she frets about the sounds to come. So far, no real worries. The only test that makes a racket is Macaroni's, and that's only because his bubbling is scribbled outside of the margins, so she will correct his by hand. She is sure he must have done much better than this little pink number tally indicates.

Ah, yes, here it is. She runs Slater's answer document through the machine, hoping it will be an improvement over his last test.

Bing, bing-bing-bing-bing. The machine sounds with the speed of a woodpecker before a long pause, then *bing-bing-bing*, followed by another long pause. She is so thrilled to see that Slater has only missed eight problems when the machine sounds two more quick *bings* in succession. Well, still, that is pretty great. Slater will be so proud when he sees he got an A.

Maybe he is growing out of his phase. Maybe Bill Daly's right, this will be the year he will learn. Maybe I am reaching him after all, Dana thinks, holding the highest of hopes.

At precisely 8:03 a.m., the children belonging to Room 14 have ignored any line formation, sorting themselves into clusters instead. They are more interested in catching up with their friends to find out who went where and did what over Thanksgiving break.

"All right, everybody, let's get you situated," Miss Burbank says with her outdoor voice but without much luck at first. "Kids, let's go; let me see you in your line, please."

"Hi, Miss Burbank," says Sibley, the first to greet her with a big smile.

"Good morning, Sibley. How was your break?"

"So much fun. We went skiing, and—" Sibley starts before she is cut off completely.

"Boys, let's go, you're on a countdown now! Five, four . . ." Miss Burbank says more forcefully this time.

"Miss Burbank, I wasn't doing anything, was I?" Neimer asks her shyly.

"No, no, not you, Neimer. I am talking to those boys who are going to make me walk all the way to the back of this line because they won't listen," Miss Burbank says, full of exasperation.

On her way, she passes Sibley, remembering they were in the middle of a conversation. "Sibley, I'm sorry, I'll be back to hear more," she says with a wink.

Sibley understands. This happens to her a lot. Anytime she has something of interest to share in a class where there are boys, somehow she always gets interrupted. Either they mock her to make her feel stupid or they bump their desks up against the back of her chair to annoy her or they talk to each other so loudly that the teacher has to put all of her attention on *them*, usually forgetting *Sibley* had something interesting to say. Poor Sibley. Her only dream is to one day go to a school with all girls so she can learn and have teachers praise her for her interesting insight.

Macaroni, Slater, Phil, and Tobey have found each other at the back of the line where none of them are supposed to be. It feels like the beginning of the school year once again, and it looks like it will require the same energy from Miss Burbank to get them settled into what should be a familiar routine by now.

"What is going on back here that you boys are not in your places on the line?" Miss Burbank asks sharply, buttoning the top collar of her long down coat.

"Nothin'," Slater says truthfully. They really weren't doing anything except finding out what each of them has for lunch today so they can figure out their trades.

"Okay then, get up to your spots so we can be ready for announcements from Mr. Daly before we go inside where it's warm," Miss Burbank says, turning to march away before spinning back around to offer, "and Slater, I think this is going to be a good day for you; don't ruin it, okay?"

The boys can only throw confused glances at each other while she escorts them back to their line number.

"The sub?" Macaroni mouths silently, wondering if this is Slater's good news.

"I don't know," Slater says, furrowing his dark, bushy eyebrows and scrunching his shoulders up high around his neck before dropping them quickly.

"Badgers, let me have your attention on this cold morning." Principal

Daly begins his morning announcements while the wind whips through his microphone, setting off ear-piercing reverb that makes all the kids put their mittens over their ears. "Do we have another mic, Mr. Simon? No? Mr. Perry, can I borrow your megaphone for just one moment? Thank you." Mr. Daly appreciatively grabs the PE teacher's favorite toy.

"Badgers, can you hear me now?"

Pitter-patter-boom-boom erupts the Badger signal for getting everyone's attention. Hundreds of children at once quickly run in place and then stomp, stomp for the five seconds it takes for them to convey they are paying attention. It is cute to witness when little kindergartners have mastered this with their teeny delicate feet, but when the whole school is doing this at the same time, it almost sounds like a stampede.

"Good job! Thank you for making it back from your Thanksgiving break. I know how happy your teachers are to see you again. I just want to remind you that we are getting ready to send out report cards soon, so to help your teachers get the time they need to work on your grades—you don't want them to send home any mistakes, right?—the school is going to have an assembly tomorrow about bullying and ways we can be nice Badgers and how we can help other Badgers who might be having a bad day to feel better so they don't hurt someone else's feelings.

"Lower-grade teachers will attend first, and your upper-grade colleagues will supervise for you; then you switch. At the end of the assembly we'll show a video called *Martin Makes a Friend.*

I think you will love it very much because Martin is a Martian coming from a faraway planet and he doesn't understand our language, and his family can't help him. When everybody laughs at how he doesn't fit in, Martin gets very sad," Principal Daly says, looking at all of the youngest students who seem focused on what will happen to Martin.

"How many of us have ever felt sad?" Principal Daly asks, raising his hand too. He sees most of the lower grades raise their hands while hugging their line partner, and he sees some of the fifth graders start to raise their hands before putting them right back down when they notice no one else in their class has a hand up. "I think Martin would love to be friends with you, too. All right, Badgers, stay warm, have a great day, and welcome back."

Room 14 scurries inside as quickly as they can, hoping the heaters that usually come on when they are not needed in August will be working today as well. "Ahhh, the heat feels so good," Neimer says, warming his little mittens on the long radiator in the back of the room.

"Move over, Neimer. We want to get some too," Slater says boisterously while Macaroni, Phil, and Tobey slide in ahead of everyone.

"Umm, you guys don't get to just hog the heater; we want some too," Kerry Ko says with ten girls standing behind her.

"We're going. We just wanted to stop here for a second," Macaroni says sheepishly to Kerry. "She thinks she's the boss of everyone," he says out of earshot.

"Well, she pretty much is," Phil says, poking Macaroni hard in the side.

"Okay, class, let's settle in, and let me start by sharing some news: good, good and bad, which do you want first?"

"Bad—" the first child shouts.

"No, good—" a few other voices say in unison.

"Wait, go good, bad, then good," Neimer calls out above the other children in disarray because they cannot make up their minds.

"I'll start with the good, then the bad, then end with the good again just for you, Neimer, how's that?" Miss Burbank begins without giving them a chance to respond. "First, you have a very good sub report from Mrs. Wilson, who—"

"She likes to be called Madame Wilson," Phil interjects enthusiastically.

"Oh, okay, well she was Mrs. Wilson to us for so long, it's hard to think of her as anything else. Anyway—" she says, unsuccessful at her attempt to continue.

"Actually, she likes it when we call her sir," Slater starts, grinning broadly at this one, and now all of the boys and some of the girls are breaking into smiles too.

"She likes to be called *sir*? Do you mean *madame*?"

"Yes, sir-madame." Slater begins the chant, which much of the class repeats good-naturedly, but since Miss Burbank is a bit confused, she is not feeling so good-natured anymore.

"Class, I don't know what little game this is, but I really want you to hear what she wrote in her report. I think it will please you as much as it pleases me, especially where three of you are concerned."

Miss Burbank continues to read the note as it is written and gives Sibley, Kerry, and Slater a few chocolate candy kisses to show her appreciation.

"Now, the bad news. I am already scheduled to attend a teacher training on Friday when we will be having our awards assembly. Would you mind if I invited back Mrs. Wilson—Madame Wilson— to distribute these awards to you on my behalf? I just don't know that I will have them done any earlier with the report cards I am still working on."

Some kids immediately nod their heads that it will be fine with them, while a few others look dejected because they were counting on getting the award and the compliment from their own teacher in front of the whole school. Still, some of the students in Room 14 look around the rows to eye each other and think this could be even more fun than the last time Madame Wilson was here.

"Fine then. And for the final bit of good news we have today," she continues with a new twinkle in her eye, pausing just for the extra second it takes to build the curiosity so high the kids lean over their desks wild with anticipation. "Your tests have been graded, and they look good!"

"Whooo-hooo! Hurray!" Cheers sound from around the room, and the kids high-five each other until someone asks the obvious question.

"Do they look good for *everybody*?" Macaroni asks hesitantly.

"They look good for *everybody*," Miss Burbank echoes back. "You all passed, and some of you did remarkably well. This might be your highest score yet," she says with a relaxed demeanor, holding the stack of tests in her arms beneath Mrs. Wilson's note. "There are a couple of you whose bubbling could not be read by the machine, but I have graded these myself and you have still passed, but please be careful to bubble within the circle next time. I am trying to teach you good habits because you might not have future teachers in middle school who will have the time to re-score sloppy work."

The kids are so anxious to see their scores, they pat each other and demur that maybe theirs won't be as good as Miss Burbank says. Maybe they got the lowest grade of all the students in the class. Their friends try to assure them that this is probably an exaggeration, but secretly they harbor the same fears. Only a handful of students know that they will be tying for first place as usual. And the drum roll begins.

"Will these ten students who obviously worked so diligently to prepare for the A they just received on this one-hundred-point test please come to the front of the room so we can celebrate you?" Miss Burbank says loudly and cheerfully.

"Kerry, Sibley, Neimer, and Vincente, please step up," she says. The class applauds. "Oh, but class, wait, there's more," she says with a fresh sparkle in her face. "Tobey, Nancy, Eliza, Momi, Ryan," she says, counting all of the children up front before she finishes, "and Slater."

There is a huge audible gasp from the two side rows where Slater and his buddies and the quiet girls surrounding them all share the same thought. *Slater? Wow, she doesn't hate him after all.*

"What? Me?" Slater says as soon as he hears his name because usually his name is only called in class when he does something wrong. While Macaroni pushes him out of his seat and Sibley steps aside to make room for him in the long line up front, Slater swings his long hair that sweeps across his eyes as if to give it a proper combing by jostling it. He gets to the front in three long steps, and in this very moment the class sees a new side to Miss Burbank.

"Class," she begins, "when you work hard, it's nice to have a little recognition. So many more of you could be up here if it just weren't for that one little, teeny, tiny oversight when you carried your numbers or forgot to double-check your equations. Remember, every point counts, right? I do want to say, though, how wonderful it is to see a few *new* faces up here, and I am especially proud to know that today," she says, while something catches in her throat and her eyes mist over, "today, we get to applaud *you*." She finishes, sweeping the back of her hand to catch the single tear dripping on her cheek before anyone can notice.

The whole class erupts in a cheerful roar of applause, which Sibley, Kerry, and Neimer mostly think is for them because they are so used to it by now. But, Macaroni and Phil are not only excited for Tobey, who has been on stage once before, they howl for Slater. Miss Burbank invites each high-scoring student to come up to her special teacher's closet where she keeps a little treat box for small class rewards. Each of them gets to choose between a small candy and a raffle ticket—which they can trade for homework passes once they collect a certain amount. The girls quickly select tickets and then take their seat.

But for Slater, this is the first time he has ever seen inside a teacher's treasure box, so he takes in all of its contents with wonder. He digs to the bottom of this satin box wrapped in purple boa feathers to find the only remaining pack of baseball cards.

"Can I have these?" he asks gently, hoping she will still honor his pick since most things are much smaller than what his fingers have discovered.

"Oh, sure, anything you want," Miss Burbank says, smiling warmly. She sees a side to Slater she has never witnessed before. He is like a small child, enchanted as if he is looking at a magical forest for the first time. Funny, she has never thought of him this innocently before.

"Cool," he says and darts back to his seat, flipping his palm up to show off his deck to Tobey, Phil, and Macaroni on his way back to his row.

When all of the kids finally settle back into their seats, even Slater's unknown enemy is still smiling after faking the sincerity behind the applause for Slater's success—because only one person saw the ink that was written on the palm of his hand before the test.

🖉   🖉   🖉   🖉

When school lets out this afternoon, Slater and his friends run the eight blocks it takes them to get home, then head inside with promises to meet up again at the park in twenty minutes after they check in with their moms.

"Hey, Mom, guess what?" Slater finds her home today working in Hank's cozy office near the living room with only one side of the French doors closed.

"Hi, honey. What's got you so excited?"

"Hi, Slater." Hank peers from around the corner while seated on the sofa, plunking away on his laptop at the side coffee table.

"Hey, Dad, you're home early," Slater says, surprised. Rarely is his dad home before dinner. *Today must be their anniversary or something, unless something bad happened at work.*

"Just home early, that's all, kiddo," Hank says mysteriously.

"Honey, what were you screaming about when you came inside? Good day at school?" Lynn asks coyly.

"Well, just look for yourself," Slater says with a big grin as he waves his test score in front of them both and hands it over.

"Slater, you got an A! This is so exciting," Lynn says brightly as she hugs her son and looks over his shoulder toward his father, to whom she gives a sly wink.

"Son, this calls for a big congratulations. Your mother and I always knew you had it in you, so we think it's about time to celebrate all of your hard work on this test!" Hank Hannigan says, lobbing the first ball over the net, waiting for his wife to hit the return.

"Honey, your father has planned something special as a way to remind you that we believe in you and we want you to keep up the good work," she says with a big Cheshire cat grin.

"How does skiing in Colorado sound for Christmas?"

"What? No way! Are you serious? That's awesome!" Slater says, still needing to be convinced that his biggest dream is really coming true. "Wait 'til I tell the guys. They are going to be so jealous! In their face!"

"Well, before you tell them, you need to decide *which* one of them you would like to invite along because we'll pay for one guest," Lynn says with a big kiss on the cheek for Hank while Slater dances around in the same spot, looking like he is stepping on firecrackers.

"No way! Oh, it's gotta be Macaroni for sure. I hope he's not going out of town too. Wow! Thanks, Mom. Thanks, Dad! This is awesome!" Slater runs out the front door again as he calls back to his parents, notifying them he will be at the park with the guys until dinner, and like a gust of wind, he is gone.

With the news of Slater's big reward turning out to be just the hit his parents expected it would be, they look smugly at each other before they burst out with laughter.

"I must say I'm glad Miss Burbank had the presence of mind to let us know in that congratulatory email that if we wanted to celebrate this little victory with an ice cream, it would be well earned," Lynn says, pleased for the heads-up.

"Yeah, I'm just glad I was able to add another seat to our flight for Macaroni before the airline was all booked," Hank says, knowing full well from Jim Peterson that this is the holiday that the two families belonging to Tobey and Phil will be vacationing together at the Petersons' ski cabin.

"Oh, when I talked to Marcy earlier, she was so excited Macaroni was going to be able to come along, this means she and Mark can plan a getaway with just the two of them because Debbie is already planning to be at her grandparents in New York for shopping."

Everything has come together nicely for Slater. His teacher has restored faith in him. His friends think he is a genius. And his parents have given him the reward of a lifetime. Good thing it's happening now because in just a few short months, Slater will not be cast as the hero in any storytelling, no matter whose version you want to believe.

CHAPTER 14

Slater Rides Again

Slater had a good week after Thanksgiving. Miss Burbank has worked tirelessly to finish her awards in time to personally give them out to her class the day *before* the assembly she will be missing. He will never forget her words when she presents his certificate, "For the Most Improved Student, and General All-Around Good Role Model." No one ever thought Miss Burbank would be calling Slater Hannigan a role model.

His friend Macaroni is equally elated, having been invited along for the Hannigans' Christmas ski trip—promising more fun than if Slater had invited Phil or Tobey. Slater even manages to convince his parents to let him and Macaroni sleep in their own adjoining room instead of staying in the family suite. The boys have fun with their many late-night shenanigans. Jumping on beds while imitating professional skiers in downhill races before crashing onto the floor of pillows as their snowbank becomes a familiar ritual the Hannigans listen to from next door—with pillows over their heads.

Once everyone settles back in for the second half of the school year, the snow keeps the town of Everly covered in a thick blanket of white. This means the days are shorter, and when darkness creeps in just after the last bus has dropped off those students staying late in the tutoring center, it feels like it should already be time for bed, still many hours away.

There is nothing to do. No one gets into any trouble because no one leaves the house. Even if you did want to go outside to throw snowballs for thirty minutes, you'd have to put on all of your snow gear and hear your mom yelling for the millionth time to keep the mudroom wiped up so somebody doesn't slip—again. Unless you play ice hockey as one of the stars of the city league's Everly Hornets, spring season for baseball tryouts feels like a million years away.

The monotony of school, home, school, home is broken only on the occasion when the school bus is stalled because the tires are spinning in two feet of fresh snow. The news channel plays every morning at dawn with kids half asleep waiting to hear if they can go back to bed because today will be a snow day. "Yippee," cheer all the kids. Unfortunately, bosses feel the opposite because they know this is when most of their employees will say they need to work from home instead of coming into the office.

When spring finally ushers in a thaw, the winter bleak that has harnessed the energy of every child cooped up for these long months is over. The hollering from indoor sledding down staircases has become exasperating.

"Time to get outside, boys," Lynn says impatiently with only half of her face put on.

"Ahhh, Mom's a monster," Graham yells swiftly, scooching backward from her vanity table in her bedroom where he is playing on the floor behind her.

"Graham, enough! Get your brother and go outside so I can leave for work," Lynn snaps.

Graham decides to run and tell Slater that Mom needs him right away and she is already counting to three. Since Slater has been on a pretty good roll with school and his parents right now, he does not want to risk being in trouble for something he has no clue about.

He runs from the kitchen where he is flipping pancakes on the griddle to surprise his mother. As soon as he comes upon her, it is he who is met with the surprise.

"Yech," he says in his first moment, seeing his mother in her half-done stage.

Lynn believes the most efficient way to put on her morning makeup is to do one side of her face completely before beginning the next. She has used one of her Crayola-looking pencils to draw a line around her whole mouth, but there is no paint inside. Her right cheek has two thick smears of pink war paint in the same way NFL players use lines, but these are not beneath her eyes. Her eyebrows have some kind of point in the middle that is usually not there when the boys wake her up from a deep sleep on Saturday mornings, and her entire eyelid is covered in green, the same as the color of a turtle's shell. The spidery things coming up from her eyeballs almost touch her eyebrows.

"Slater, how can I help you?"

"Yeesh, Mom, you look like a gargoyle clown," Slater says, alarmed.

"Gargoyle clown, that's a good one," Graham says, rolling around on the bed.

"Slater, I'm getting ready for work. Take Graham and go play outside. It's going to be a nice day."

"What did you want?" Slater says, puzzled by the fast motion she makes switching between brushes and paints to start the other side of her face.

"When?" Lynn Hannigan says with her mouth open wide, tugging off her fake eyelashes to reinsert them again with less glue this time.

"Mom, Graham said you needed me," Slater says, pushing again because he can't stand to see her poking a drawing pencil around the inside part of her eye.

"Slater, I don't know what you're talking about, but I am busy here," Lynn says, carefully trying to finish her look by dusting her face with a big fat brush dipped in powder that creates a cloud around her.

"Graham said—"

Slater turns around to see Graham pulling back his head from where he has been spying from around the corner. He is down on all fours creeping like a Ninja to see what Mom will say to Slater.

Neeeeeeehhhhhhh! All of the sudden a piercing alarm sounds downstairs in the kitchen. Smoke has already filled the adjacent living room and begun to hover at the bottom of the staircase. Lynn stumbles past her boys who are scrambling to find out what is on fire and asking incessantly if the fire trucks are going to come.

"Slaaaater, what's burning?"

"Nothing, Mom. I was just making you surprise pancakes and then Graham said you wanted to see me."

Grabbing the dining room chair and dragging it to stand beneath the smoke alarm in the hallway adjacent to the kitchen, Lynn stands as high on her tippy toes as she can to smack the exterior of the alarm with the handle of her wooden spoon.

Ring, ring, the telephone interrupts urgently. *Ring, ring*, to eager cries from Graham of, "I'll get it."

"Boys, don't answer the phone," Lynn screams over the blaring alarm that has both of her sons covering their ears with their hands.

"Hello? Yes, this is Lynn Hannigan. The password is Mount Vesuvius"—a joke she and Hank had between them after Slater wreaked havoc as an overactive toddler pulling down closet rods for low-hanging skirts or toilet brushes he would use to scrub the cars or every kitchen pot he would pull out before he could hide inside the cupboard.

"I can barely hear you. I am trying to deactivate it now. Can you hold on?"

But before she is able to put down the phone, the operator wants to know if a fire station should be dispatched.

"No, no, it's just smoke from some burned pancakes; nothing more, no flames."

The operator agrees to hold until Lynn can grab the broom handle where instead of gently trying to untwist the lid to reveal the battery inside and disconnecting it, she destroys that plastic disc until its cover is dangling from the wires above—with the alarm still fully screaming throughout the neighborhood.

She bats at the wires until finally they come apart from the hold they have on the battery pack, which falls to the ground before skating across the floor.

Silence, at last. She returns to the phone to say, "Thank you for holding. Everything is under control now. Appreciate it." She hangs up quickly and surveys the scene.

Her flowered oven mitts that are supposed to be fire retardant are creating so much smoke that she can't stop the smoldering even when dousing them under water. "Slater, take these outside," she says, putting both oven mitts that were left on the griddle to be carted away on a cookie sheet. She instructs Slater to take the bag of flour and pour it all over the mitts in the garden outside, which seems to do the trick.

"Good grief, what a mess," she says, looking at Graham, who looks back at her with his arms folded in the same way his mother stands now.

"Slater, come inside. I appreciate the gesture, but you have to be really careful in the kitchen, honey. Accidents in the bathroom and the kitchen always turn into something a lot worse that could have been avoided in the first place. Think ahead," Lynn says, scolding gently.

"I know, Mom, but I can open the front door and windows to clear out the smoke and air out the house," he says, trying to be helpful.

"Look, I need you to clean all of this up, every single thing, because I have to finish getting ready and I'm running late," Lynn says, looking at Slater while wrapping her arm around the back side of Graham, who is scurrying off to watch TV.

"No, mister, you are just as much a part of this for distracting your brother," she says, corralling Graham in front of her. "You be sure to do half the cleanup in here. Slater will tell you what to do while I go finish upstairs."

"See, that's what you get, Graham. You're so lucky the house didn't burn down. That woulda been all your fault," Slater says, spitefully harassing Graham.

"It's not all my fault, stupid Slater," Graham says, starting to cry.

"Oh, brother, not this again," Slater says, trying to show more compassion this time. "Graham, stop with the tears, all right? Here, just put the furniture back and take out this garbage and I'll do the rest," Slater offers peaceably.

Graham shuffles behind the dining room chair, pushing it slowly across the hardwood floors, sniveling all the way. It won't be until his mother notices the scratch through the hallway that he will really have something to cry about later.

✐   ✐   ✐   ✐

Several weeks go by, and just as students are beginning to make plans for their spring break, Slater is making plans for his big birthday splash to take place the week before vacation.

"Slater, what kind of theme do you want this year?" Lynn asks, with Graham within earshot.

"Not robots. That's what I'm picking for my theme, Slater," Graham calls out.

"Dude, umm, I will not be picking robots. That is the last kind of party my friends want to come to," he says, razzing Graham.

"Mom, Slater says my party's stupid. Tell him he's being mean again," Graham says, lying on his stomach, cupping his chin in his hands while he watches his favorite cartoons before school.

"Okay, so not robots. What *do* you want? I need to start making reservations if we're having it at a restaurant again like that jungle theme last year," Lynn says with her computer open, ready to do a search as soon as Slater gives her an idea.

"I want to do a cowboy theme, but like at a real ranch where we can ride real horses, not ponies, and where all my friends from class can come, and I want rodeo clowns. Oh, and I want a gun fight with a real bad guy to show up in a black hat and scare everybody like they're getting robbed and stuff. Oh, and I want to be the sheriff, and I think I need a badge and a holster," Slater says, reeling off idea after idea, obviously having thought about this for quite some

time. "Oh, and maybe you could get me a real BB gun this time."
Slater breathes for a minute.

"Oh my, a cowboy theme," Lynn says, already trying to imagine a
large enough place where she can accommodate Slater's classmates
and get enough horses. "That sounds pretty fun. I think I can make a
lot of this happen, but let me make some calls today and I'll let you
know more after school. Slater, what do you want for your cake?"

"I want it to be chocolate on the inside and I want it to look like a
big western showdown on top, like have them decorate so there are
saloon buildings and two cowboys getting ready to have a gunfight,
and all the buildings could be like gingerbread houses where we
get to eat them. But I don't want actual gingerbread. What can the
baker make instead? That's what I want," Slater says, breathless.

"Okay, I'll figure something out. I have a pretty clear idea of what
you want," Lynn says, smiling at her cowboy.

"Thanks, Mom," Slater says, heading upstairs to brush his teeth.

"Hey, wait, Slater, one more thing," she calls after him as he pivots
on the middle step and leans halfway down the banister.

"What?"

"What do you want to do for your invitations?"

"Oh, I know, you could have a horse with a bad guy ride up to
school, and out of the saddlebag, there could be, like, these wanted
posters with each of my friends' faces and the details of the party.
Oh man, that would be so cool. Everybody would want to come
for sure," Slater says, getting carried away with his imagination.

"Okay, sheriff, I'll see what I can do, but I'm pretty sure there's got to be a rule about horses coming to school," Lynn says with a smirk. "And hey, Slater, we can't have a class party without inviting all of the class, so this one is not just your *friends*, you understand?" Lynn says slowly while the doomed expression on Slater's face sinks in.

"No way, Mom. I do not want Sibley White at my party. No way. She's turned into such a weirdo. No one even likes her except for the kids who think they know it all too."

"Well, Slater, if it's a class party, it's got to be the whole class. That's the way we work the birthday circuit; you know this," Lynn says matter-of-factly.

"But I don't even go to some of those kids' parties; why do they have to come to mine?" Slater says adamantly.

"Sweetheart, some of those kids aren't having parties; that's why you're not going. Believe me, I know what's going on in the neighborhood. So this is your chance to offer some fun to those kids who rarely get invited to anything," Lynn says sweetly.

"Mom, noooo. Sibley White is way too embarrassing, and I don't want people to think I'm friends with her. She can't come. I don't care who else you invite, but I don't want a party if Sibley White has to be there," Slater says, running the rest of the way upstairs and slamming the bathroom door loudly behind him.

"Who's Cindy White?" Graham says, catching only pieces of their conversation but fully paying attention now that Slater's screaming about some girl.

"Her name is Sibley, honey. I don't know her, but she's one

of Slater's classmates, that's all," Lynn says, trying to steer the conversation away from all the reasons Slater does not want her at his party.

"But why can't she come to Slater's party?"

"I don't think that's the case, Graham, but it's nothing you need to worry about today. Just do me a favor and don't bug your brother about this, okay, buddy?" Lynn says finally, reaching down to give her little man a hug. "Now, go upstairs and get dressed, and when Slater comes out of the bathroom, I want you to go brush your teeth, and do a good job today, okay?"

"K, Mom," Graham says as he bustles up the staircase taking the steps two at a time, or at least trying. Since his legs aren't that long yet, he misses the second set and spills forward, bumping his head on the carpet runner protecting the hardwood stairs. He looks around to see if anybody saw him before determining if now is a good time to cry. Nope, nobody there. He bounds up the rest one at a time and doesn't even feel the bump growing on his forehead.

Dear Miss Burbank,

I see that my appointed time for my volunteer hour will be this Friday. Is it all right with you if I bring my uncle who will be in town to also help out in class?

Thanks very much,
Lynn Hannigan, mother of Slater Hannigan

When Miss Burbank finds this email, nothing indicates that she should imagine anything out of the ordinary, so she replies that yes, of course, Slater's great-uncle is also welcome in class, and there will be two passes waiting for Mrs. Hannigan in the front office upon checking in.

Poor Miss Burbank. She never saw it coming. When Lynn Hannigan shows up to school, she certainly does have her uncle in tow. However, since he is just parking the car, he will be arriving a few minutes behind her and she will bring his visitor's badge to the classroom where they will meet. Little does anyone suspect that this southern gentleman is also part of a show that will soon begin in Room 14.

"Okay, everybody, today we have Slater's mother, Mrs. Hannigan, and her uncle—so he would be Slater's great-uncle—to help you with your center work today. I'd like group one to work on spelling workbooks up to chapter twenty-eight today. Group two, I need you to—"

"Howdy folks," a deep sprawling accent from the south gives a hearty hello. "I'm Sheriff Brady, and I'm not just here to help you with your project today, I'm here to tell you about a villain we're trying to round up in these parts of town," he says in character to all of the kids who have their mouths open agape. "You may have seen him, but I doubt it because he sure is slick, but we think we have a trap set for him and we need to count on you fine citizens to help us bring this rascal to justice."

With this introduction, Sheriff Brady unrolls a poster he has hidden behind his back secured by his belt. It reads: Wanted—Room 14 classmates—to meet at high noon at the O.K. Corral for a showdown that is not to be missed. Sheriff Slater and his deputies will bring Wild Kid McKidd the Cowboy Killer to justice. Plenty of ponies and cake to go around. "Now who wants to get deputized? I've got an engraved invitation badge for each of you with your name on it."

All of the hands shoot up wildly in the air. While Miss Burbank has barely had a minute to take in this spectacle, Lynn quickly gives handfuls of badges to the kids nearest to her for them to help pass out, and so does Uncle Van. The speech only takes five minutes, but the image of Sheriff Brady lasts all day. The kids will tell their friends at lunch how scared they were when they saw this huge man walk in with a ten-gallon white cowboy hat and a big gold badge on his jacket lapel, and the monstrous buckle he wore low beneath his oversized belly.

"Dude, that was awesome!" Macaroni says, not even knowing that Slater had this planned the whole time.

"Yeah, he really looks like a real cowboy, too! Hey, who is Kid McKidd?" Phil asks curiously.

"Oh, man, just you wait. You gotta see the show my mom has planned. It's gonna be super awesome this year," Slater says, shoveling chips into his face, smearing his orange fingers on his jeans instead of using the napkin inside his bag.

"That poster was so cool; who drew that? It looks just like an old-time real-life Wanted poster, especially the part where all of our names were in the box under Wanted," Macaroni says.

"I don't know. I just told my mom what theme I wanted, and you know her, she just makes it all happen, I guess," Slater says, pulling a few french fries from Tobey's plate.

"So everybody's invited, cool," Phil says casually.

"Hey, I guess this means that Sibley's coming too—it's the whole class, right?" Tobey asks, full well knowing this will provoke a reaction from Slater.

"I don't even want her to come, she's so weird," Slater protests and then drinks his carton of chocolate milk in one big, long gulp. "I hope she doesn't show up. She'd just ruin everything, and I know nobody else is gonna want her there."

"Dude, I would die if she had to come to my party," Tobey says, as if this is the worst situation ever.

"What are you gonna do? Can't you just talk to your mom one more time? Have her talk to maybe Sibley's mom about maybe Sibley should stay home." Macaroni thinks as hard as he can, but even this idea doesn't sound like it will work.

"Dude, you have no idea. I totally told my mom I didn't even want to have this party if she had to be invited, but no-oh, my mom said we're not about to stop having parties on account of one weird kid," Slater says in a mocking tone.

"Man, I hope she doesn't show up," Phil says, thinking of another plan. "Hey, maybe she'll be sick that day, maybe it will rain and she'll be, like, outside playing and she'll get all drenched and then she'll get the flu," he says, unable to even convince himself it could happen.

"Guess you're kinda stuck, huh?" Macaroni says, sorry-like.

"Guess I am," Slater agrees dejectedly, "unless someone wants to give Sibley the impression that maybe she's not real wanted at the party, maybe then she'll stay home," Slater says, perking right up.

"Oh, I don't know, I hate to see girls cry. You know what my mom would do to me if she found out I was ever mean to a girl?" Macaroni says fearfully.

"Yeah, I can't do it either, Slater. That's just too mean. I wouldn't even know what to say to her." Phil bows out cowardly.

"Well, I could drop a small hint, like, maybe wouldn't she rather be doing something artful like instead of hanging around a bunch of horses in the dust when she could be going to, like, a museum, or something," Tobey offers, trying to be helpful.

"Hey, yeah, that's real good, trying to give her something else she might really be more interested in doing. I like that," Slater says, feeling more encouraged now. "Can you look for some things going on in town April 14th so that she can be somewhere else?" Slater finishes, feeling like this is a good plan.

"Okay, I'll look into it. Trust me, she won't even get suspicious; I'll be real sly," Tobey says in a whisper so nobody else even five seats away can hear their secret plan for ousting Sibley White from attending the O.K. Corral.

For the next week, the fifth graders from Room 14 are all abuzz at the excitement planned for Slater's cowboy-themed party. Lynn has reserved the Dusty Darn Tootin' Ranch that runs parties to please any pocketbook. She is so impressed with their variety of optional add-ons for the ultimate cowboy experience that she ends up choosing the most expensive party package called The Showdown. The Dusty Darn Tootin' Ranch has enough acreage to stage an old-fashioned holdup. Their own little motorized train runs along tracks through the wooded grove where passengers are transported to the picnic area. While the conductor plays tour guide, he cautions the good folks—which are all of Slater's classmates—all about the tales of Kid McKidd the Cowboy Killer who is still on the loose.

During these minutes of convincing role-play, the train whistle blows feverishly in the same moment a black horse charges up to the open-air windows. The villain Kid McKidd the Cowboy Killer is dressed in a black hat, black shirt, black pants, and black boots. He jumps dramatically from his horse and grabs at the rail, swinging himself over it with ease as if he has done this a thousand times before—which he has. He pulls down the black handkerchief tied behind his ears to cover his face, and as soon as he does, the passengers always know that they will never be left alive once they have witnessed the robber up close.

Then he begins from his well-rehearsed script. "As many of you may have heard tell, I am Kid McKidd, infamous bank robber and cowboy killer, but I saw y'all on this here train and figgered since town's got sheriff and deputies out lookin' fer me, I'd come collect my loot from you nice people." Sure enough, the passengers, who never expected to be robbed today, squeal and tear up.

Kid McKidd holds out his long-nosed black pistol and twirls it around his index finger a few impressive times, then points it straight and gives instructions. "Put up yer hands and nobody'll get hurt. Conductor, I'd like you to offer yer hat to all these gents and ladies to empty out their wallets and purses," he says real sweetly before changing his tune. "Be sure that that there hat is overflowing by the time you come back because I'd hate to think some of these nice folks here are holdin' out on Kid McKidd."

"Eeek!" says one lady with a diamond gem dangling from her necklace before she faints directly onto the picnic basket she is holding in her arms.

"Conductor, that's where you start," Kid McKidd says, pointing to the lady now in a clump as the conductor does what he's told and rushes to rip the necklace from her throat before she awakens.

"No, no, I can't allow you to hurt my family," says a brave father of four from the middle bench seat as he stands in the aisle while his wife protests his exposure.

"Well, I sure am sorry to hear this bad news, sir. Take that," Kid McKidd says as he empties out his gun into the man's feet, forcing him to dance like a little circus performer. "You see, yer dancin' fer me already, sir, and you look like yer actually havin' a pretty good time," Kid McKidd says as the man begs for him to stop and offers him his wallet and his own wife's silk purse.

"Now, that's what bank lendin' is all about. 'Preciate yer co-operation." Kid McKidd sidles up to the man to accept his treasures before stuffing them into the conductor's hat himself. "Pleasure doin' business with you today."

The excitement builds as the first of the passengers has been robbed. A thunderous pounding can be heard at the front of the train. Running alongside, at warp speed, is a white stallion carrying atop it a man in a white cowboy hat—crouching as he steadies himself for the jump he is about to make onto the train. He comes from behind Kidd McKidd's view so only the passengers can see what is about to take place.

To the side, Kid McKidd sees the stallion charge off alone with only an empty saddle and realizes his fate is about to be met.

"Turn around, you yella-bellied coward," the good guy in the white hat says slowly, pointing his gun straight at Kid McKidd's back.

"You'll never take me alive, I warn you," Kid McKidd says, turning abruptly to fire blanks that sound convincingly real as the good guy fires back more of the same.

While Kid McKidd lies in a heap upon the floor, the good guy makes sure the conductor is all right and that no one else is injured. As he says his fond farewell to the passengers and the women who swoon over being rescued by such a handsome cowboy, the man in white professes his gratitude to the Dusty Darn Tootin' Ranch for allowing him to play here one more weekend. He thanks his fellow passengers who were in on the act and hopes the partygoers today have a real good time.

Everyone on board erupts into an earth-shattering applause as kids say to each other how real they thought this was and how scared they were they'd never make it home alive.

This alone is worth the price of admission, as far as Lynn is concerned. But, there is more fun to be had for Slater Hannigan's guests. They are given thirty minutes each to ride the stallion of their choice outside of the corral, up and down a long trail and sometimes even breaking into a spirited run for just a minute. The cake looks just like Slater described, and there is so much of it that each guest is able to have two slices.

Roasting hot dogs and marshmallows and learning how to shoot at cans from real honest-to-goodness cowboys is fun, sure. But even better, as a goody bag gift, every kid gets to take home their own authentic cowboy hat. Girls get white ones. Boys get black ones. It is the most special birthday party anyone has ever attended. Slater gets to be the little sheriff all day long and has fun arresting his friends for small infractions like drinking too much punch.

The offenders then have to give him something in return to get out of jail, like a promise to lick his boots—which they gladly make since those boots are new from the box, displayed on his gift table with slathers of chocolate frosting on the bottom of both heels. Or, he might make them eat from a bucket of worms, which is really just gummy worm candy that they like anyway.

Yep, it was a perfect party. The only thing that made it a million times better than it could have been is what happened when his doorbell rang *two hours before* Slater was supposed to leave for the Dusty Darn Tootin' Ranch with his family. Lynn answered it, surprised by the guest in her doorway.

"Slater, would you mind coming down here for a minute please, honey? There is someone here to see you."

No, it was not Sibley White. It was her mother.

"Happy birthday, Slater. Unfortunately, Sibley woke up sick this morning and she is so sorry she won't be able to make it to your party, but she wanted you to have this." Her mother looked Slater in the eyes earnestly while she spoke her words softly and sincerely.

A huge wash of relief came over Slater, followed by a small tinge of guilt—followed by another feeling of victory that everything worked out for him—again.

"Gee, thanks," Slater said, reaching eagerly for the box that was already wrapped in paper featuring western-themed boots and cartoon cows wearing sheriff badges. "Tell Sibley I'm sorry. I hope she feels better and that I really appreciate it."

He hoped by *it* she knew he meant *the gift*. He didn't want Sibley's mother to think he appreciated Sibley not showing up, even though this is what he secretly wished for when he blew out his family birthday cake at last night's dinner.

As far as anyone knew, it was completely Tobey's idea to disinvite Sibley. Anytime anyone ever asked Slater if that's what he wanted, he played it off like anyone could come to his party; it was for the whole class. Somehow, *someone* just didn't believe him.

CHAPTER 15

The Party's Over

Slater could not have been more surprised when he tore through
the wrapping of Sibley's present before leaving for his epic birthday
party at the Dusty Darn Tootin' Ranch. Inside this gigantic box that
Sibley's mother carried in her two outstretched arms is a tiny replica
of a western town—a build-your-own model using easy-to-follow
directions. It has all the parts needed for erecting saloons, an old
jail, a general post office, and hotels. It also comes complete with
horses and little people you can dress in any number of costumes
already included. It will probably take the entire summer to put
together with a little patience and a lot of glue. To keep it safe, after
it is all finished, a glass hood goes over the whole production so
everything can be viewed but not ruined by younger human hands.

Every time Slater looks at this gift, he gets a sick feeling in the
pit of his tummy. *Why did she go and get me a present at all?*

Why is it such a cool one? Was she really sick or was she faking? These are the only thoughts Slater can manage before he goes to the party. Once he is at the Dusty Darn Tootin' Ranch, he forgets all about Sibley, but as soon as he comes home, there it is—*that* gift staring him in the face again.

He didn't mention any of this to his friends earlier today. He just wants to think about what it could mean. *Is it supposed to mean something? Is this some kind of a trick?* Slater can't figure it out, so he finally goes to sleep.

The next morning, he is ready for target practice in the backyard— wearing his new cowboy boots—to hit the cans sitting on the wood stumps his dad chopped for him. His new BB gun is just what he's always wanted, and he still can't believe what an awesome party he had yesterday.

"Hey, cowboy, where you headed?" his mom asks him over her coffee and the morning paper.

"Dad and I are going shootin'," he says eagerly.

"Well, I think you've got about thirty-four thank-you notes to start writing. Go get your good pens and come on down here," Lynn says without looking up. "As soon as you get the first ten done, you and Dad can go shootin'," she says, imitating him lovingly.

"But, Mom, there's no wind right now and—"

"Slater, we all had a big day yesterday, so I expect you to keep the whining to a minimum and do as I say, or I will start taking away some of your new toys and donating them to children who *will* appreciate them."

He knows she means it, too.

"Yes, ma'am."

After Slater writes his thank-you notes on his cowboy-themed cards, he finally gets to shoot at about fifty cans with his dad. Fortunately, Graham is off playing with his own friends so he and his dad get to spend some quality time alone.

"Hey, Dad, where'd you learn to shoot so good?"

"Something Grandpa taught me when I was a kid. We lived in a small town, and sometimes Grandpa would take me out where there was some land and ask me if I thought I could shoot a squirrel from a tree. As soon as I did, after about eight million tries, we had squirrel stew for dinner that weekend. Your grandmother seasoned it so it tasted just like chicken. She added in carrots and celery and put it on the stove to boil for hours."

"Oh, gross, I think I'm going to be sick, Dad," Slater says as he bends over dry heaving. "Seriously, don't tell me anything else."

"Okay, son, you all right?" Hank asks gently before confirming what he has always known. "Bud, you never would have survived the way I grew up. You are way too much of a city boy, and I think we've spoiled you rotten," Hank says, half teasing.

"Yeah, there's no way I would ever eat squirrel stew, not even if I was starving in the middle of a desert," he says, still half bent over with his eyes watering.

"That's good, because if you were in the desert, you'd have to eat snake; squirrels only live in the woods," his dad says, slapping him on the back before they return inside.

By the time Slater mows the lawn and dusts his and Graham's rooms, his two Sunday chores, and finishes another twenty-four thank-you notes, it is time for dinner, then bed. He is sacked out. He stretches out under his covers and looks at the moon peeking in through his shutters. Its beams reflect their light off of his encased cowboy town that still needs to be built. He realizes he cannot go to sleep just yet.

He sneaks downstairs to rummage through his backpack where all of his thank-you notes are bundled together with the ribbon his mother gave him to find the one he wrote to Sibley. When he pulls it from the stack, its corners bend beneath the tie, giving it a broken, crinkled appearance now. No matter. When he gets back to his room, he rips it up into fourteen pieces and tosses it into his garbage.

Dear Sibley, he starts again on a new notecard. *I want to say sorry that you missed my birthday party. It wasn't the same without you there.* Well, this part is the truth. *I keep looking at your cool gift and I just wanted to say thanks because it's pretty awesome. I am sure building this model will take me all summer. But it will be fun. Hey, sorry you were sick. Oh wait, I said that part. See you at school. From, Slater Hannigan, Room 14.*

He likes it better than his first two drafts, so he takes it back downstairs to tie it up with the others.

At school the next day, Slater is greeted by many different versions of, "Yee-haw, darn-tootin', and stick 'em up cowboy," from his classmates who are already standing on their number spots.

All he can do is high-five everyone as he goes down the line. Thank goodness Sibley isn't here yet. He thinks she'll feel much better once she reads his note.

Miss Burbank arrives and greets her class cheerily on this bright and beautiful Monday morning. They all listen to Principal Daly make his usual morning announcements, this time adding in notes about rules for attending the fun end-of-the-year celebration events. "Behavior and grades are your minimum requirements. Please be sure you are doing everything a good Badger should in order to end your year on a bright note," he finishes with a hearty clap, signaling that students should all follow their teachers into their rooms now.

The morning continues without anything out of the ordinary happening. But at recess, when Slater is passing out all of his thank-you notes, the only person he cannot find is Sibley White. Where is Sibley White? She is not in the cafeteria buying hot cocoa or yogurt. She is not on the playground playing four-square with the other girls. She is not in the library hiding out with all of her other friends—the books—and she is not hanging out with Miss Burbank in the classroom because when Slater runs past the opened door real fast, he sees only Miss Burbank alone, reading at her desk.

He decides he better hold on to Sibley's note for when he sees her in person and thinks this will probably be at lunch. During class, he tries to get her attention, but she keeps her hair covered over her eyes now that her bangs have grown so long she can hardly make eye contact with anyone, including Miss Burbank.

In fact, if anyone had been paying attention, they would have noticed that Sibley White had pretty much turned invisible. Even for the easy questions Miss Burbank asks in class, Sibley never raises her hand anymore. When she sees her teacher taking long pauses away from her lesson to glance her way, hoping Sibley will participate, Sibley will wait until someone else has already been called upon before she pretends like her hand was going to be raised.

When Slater does find Sibley standing at the end of the lunch line, he rushes up to her before meeting up with his friends who are saving him a seat. "Hey, Sibley, hey, I just wanted to give you this thank-you note I wrote—"

As soon as he says the words with his hand outstretched, she grabs the envelope from his fingers and tears it in half and then in half again and throws the whole mess on the cafeteria floor. She walks hastily toward the exit and never looks back. She spends the rest of her lunchtime crying in the bathroom stall all by herself.

"Girls! What's their deal? I just tried to give her my thank-you note and she tore it all up," Slater says, completely baffled.

"Umm, we know, we saw," Macaroni says with his mouth completely full of a vegetarian delight sandwich with extra alfalfa sprouts his mother made especially for him.

"Just trying to be a nice guy and look what it gets me," Slater says, waving his hand behind him in the direction Sibley last stood as if he could care less about Sibley and her stupid tantrum.

"Eh, whatever is bugging her is not your problem, man," Phil says, sounding more and more like his divorced father.

Convinced Slater has nothing further to worry about, he goes on about his day in class as if Sibley White simply does not exist. It is not exactly hard to pretend she is not there; he no longer works in a group with her ever since Miss Burbank started mixing up the class teams months ago.

The weekdays pretty much fall away as Slater lives for weekends when he can go to his baseball games and hit his homeruns to chanting crowds who usually say to each other, "That boy has done it again."

If his father happens to be at one of his games, Slater can usually hear a familiar roar, before the enthusiastic encouragement of, "That a boy, run, run, run!" And on these days when Hank Hannigan is in the stands, Slater never disappoints.

As the school year finally winds down, Miss Burbank gives her class exactly thirty minutes to clean out their desks, including checking in the textbooks that were assigned to them at the beginning of the year. When they think they are done, they need their buddy to double check that all of the sterilizing and wiping down has been done thoroughly.

Sibley White has emptied out her desktop completely. She props open the lid, using the kickstand to keep it from slamming shut unexpectedly, the way Miss Burbank demonstrated on the first day of school. She has placed all of the items she is discarding neatly on the left side of her foot and everything she is keeping tucked carefully into her backpack. While she unpacks every last item, Sibley White is unaware of the attention she has been receiving from one curious onlooker in the next row.

Slater cannot believe his eyes when he sees the red-tipped paintbrush that has dried without ever being washed. What Sibley White does not know is that she has unwittingly forgotten to keep this clue hidden inside her science journal where it has been tucked out of sight ever since she painted that paper bag bearing Slater's fate. *How could it have been Sibley when she left the Halloween Haunt early because she was too afraid to stay?* Slater wondered. *Could it be possible this brush was used for something else? Maybe she is holding it for the real culprit?* Slater has no idea, but he tortures himself with these questions and knows he must confront her after school to get his answer.

Instead of bringing Macaroni or any of the other guys with him, Slater decides to follow Sibley home, staying back just far enough to avoid drawing any suspicion to himself. In the five blocks it takes to walk the opposite direction of how he goes home, he sees up ahead of him a group of bigger boys playing keep-away with something. Another block closer and Slater recognizes that it is a little black cat they are tossing between each other like a ball. As soon as Slater hears shrieks of despair, he runs faster than he ever has around four diamond bases.

"Leave my cat alone! Help, someone! Give him back to me," Sibley says, beside herself with hot tears coming out of her eyes while her red-faced shouting does little good against these bullies.

"What, this mangy old thing? We like cats. Don't you worry, we're gonna make him our cat now," the biggest boy says with a chuckle.

Plow! Bam! Boom! Slater doesn't even wait to ask what their plans are or to take the precious minutes negotiating the release of the cat hostage. He just slams into the crowd of three like he is diving into home. He grabs their ankles as he goes down and they all topple over each other. Snickers the cat knows to jump high onto the tree limb above, but not before letting out a yowl and leaving a few deep scratches in his predator's freckled face.

As soon as the boys figure out what hit them, they all rise at once, threatening to pound Slater into the ground. "Go ahead and lay a finger on me, I dare you! My dad's the district attorney, and he'll have you in jail so fast for harassment, your head will spin," Slater says powerfully. "And then I'm gonna send the animal rights activists to your house—we'll see how your parents like it when you're all over the news for torturing animals," Slater says, throwing out the worst thing he can think to say.

"Dude, calm down, we were just trying to rescue her cat from the tree, you totally misunderstood," the tallest one says, backing up from the group. "Anyway, I gotta get home to do my homework," he says, bolting before he can be held liable for anything else.

"Yeah, you losers better get outta here now because I'm pretty sure the neighbors on this block are already calling my dad's office, and there'll probably be squad cars here any minute to take you into juvy," Slater shouts down the street, hoping the bullies can still hear the last of his words as they turn the corner.

"Slater, wow! Where'd you come from? I didn't even see you," Sibley says before crying hysterically. "I-I did-n't want them hur-hurting my cat." The sniveling grows into a full wail now. "I-I don't-on't know wa-why they are always picking on meeee." Snot runs down from her nose, and her painful expression and high-pitched voice signal she must need a tissue, but the best Slater can offer is the tail from his long, plaid shirt. "I hate-ate those kids." Big gulps of air come in and out of Sibley now as she tries to calm herself down. "They're so-so meeeean." And then it starts again from the beginning—the wailing, the sniveling, the eyes shut so tight it is a wonder any leakage of tears can seep through.

"Sibley, it's okay, they're gone now," Slater says reassuringly. "If you want me to go inside and make a report to my dad's office, I can tell your parents I was a witness, and I am sure the police can easily figure out who these kids are; probably they've done this before," Slater says, seeming to know an awful lot about the law.

"Well, I guess it would be all right. I don't know if my parents are home yet, but I know the names of those boys because they live around the corner, so if you want to call your dad, it's okay by me," Sibley says, able to stifle her tears finally as she turns to lead Slater to her front door.

It isn't every day that kids get invited to peek inside Sibley White's house. There are always rumors about what goes on behind the weathered exterior of crooked shutters and why people rarely see the family. Sibley doesn't mind. She is pretty amused by the ridiculous stories kids can make up that couldn't be further from the truth. Sure, she likes to come home instead of hanging out with other kids after school. After all, much more interesting things await her once she walks up the rickety stairs to her three-story house. It doesn't matter to her that her family never takes an interest in fixing up the peeling paint, or even trimming the overgrown weeds that plague her front windows. As far as Sibley is concerned, it means more privacy and fewer peepers dying to know what happens beyond her front door. Oh, if they only knew.

And on this day, one such lucky kid gets the chance to find out. His name is Slater, and Sibley thinks he's been especially kind to rescue her mangy little cat from those mean neighborhood boys. On their way inside, she offers him some cookies and milk, leaving him there alone in the living room. He peers straight into an open book clearly marked with notes in the margin. He learns something new that day, and now it explains the odd collection housed inside the glass bookcase standing directly in front of him.

In the time it takes for Sibley to return from the kitchen, Slater has discovered her family's secret.

"Slater, that book is not meant for your eyes," Sibley says rather curtly. "My parents are rather private, and I don't think they would be comfortable knowing I have an unexpected guest."

"So this explains it, Sibley—"

"Slater, not another word. We cannot have this conversation here because everything is being recorded," she says without turning her head, trying to indicate with her eyes the cameras in the corners of the room behind her.

"Sibley," Slater starts, not knowing how he should say what he has come to say now that he just rescued her cat. "I think I know another secret about you that doesn't have to do with any of this here," he says, eyeing the bookcase in her living room.

"Slater, that makes us even, because if you think you've got a secret on me, I've got an even bigger one on you." Slater did not see this coming. *What could it be? What could Sibley White possibly have on me?*

"Well, then by all means, ladies first," Slater says slowly, not sure if he should be afraid of what Sibley White thinks she knows.

"Oh, no, Slater, I think *you* should go first. You obviously followed me home for some important reason. Grateful as I am you were here, I am sure it is not because you were out doing cat patrol," Sibley says with a sly grin.

"Okay, Sibley. Here's what I want to know. I saw you today in class. You were emptying out all of your things from your desk, one by one—and I saw it," Slater says as if this should be enough of a clue to force Sibley into confession right then and there.

"Slater, I need a little more. What are you even talking about?"

"Sibley, I saw that old red paintbrush." No response. No expression. Stone cold features only.

"Slater, what are you *saying*?"

"You wrote my fate on that bag and hung it outside of our classroom after the Halloween Haunt, didn't you?"

"So, we're being honest here now, is that what we're supposed to be doing?"

"Why'd you do it, Sibley? What did I ever do to you?"

"Oh, huh! Slater Hannigan, what *haven't* you done to me? You are the meanest boy in school, and you know it. You thrive on that. You don't care who gets hurt, and you especially don't care if it's me," Sibley says, raising her voice and forgetting to breathe in between her cutting words.

He can see the flush in her cheeks and the splotches of pink appearing on her neck. He can also see the steaming tears welling again in her eyes, and this is why he is so glad he doesn't have sisters. *Why do girls always cry when they are mad and sad and happy?*

"But, here's what I don't get—you left that Halloween party *early*, so how could you have known what the witch said at the *end*?"

"Slater, you don't pay attention to anyone but yourself. You are mean and selfish, and I don't know why I am the only girl in class you like to make fun of. There are plenty of other girls who are just as smart, or just as weird, or just as something else. Why don't you pay some attention to them sometime and share your nastiness around?" Sibley says so fast she spits because her retainer keeps slipping.

"Geesh, Sibley, I'm sorry. I didn't even know you knew—well, what I mean to say is I didn't know you were upset," Slater says, starting to feel bad.

"And to think I've kept your secret when all I needed to do was say it to the right person and your whole life would be changed—for the worse, Slater—for the worse!" Sibley turns her back on him and asks him to leave.

"Wait, Sibley. What are you talking about? What secret?"

"That day we took our big test with Madame Wilson there? I

saw your hand," Sibley says, looking for an immediate reaction from Slater.

"You saw my hand?" Slater says, fumbling, wondering how he is going to explain this one.

"Yeah, I saw your hand with notes that would be on the test. I saw it when you reached forward to borrow my striped tangerine-and-lime pencil. Madame Wilson never caught you because, lucky you, she gave us all privacy folders. And then you got your name called to come up with me for your A on the test. Do you think that's fair, Slater? Some of us have to work really hard, and we don't like to be in the same company as cheaters." Sibley has said it all now. There is nothing left. They can finish the last week of school and then never see each other again—until next year in middle school.

"Sibley, you're right, but I want you to know that the truth is, I wrote notes about stuff I actually knew and just didn't want to forget. I swear, I wasn't cheating. I *knew* it. I just get really nervous on tests. We're not all super smart like you, Sibley. Things don't always come even after the third and fourth time we have to study it. I promise you, I never had to use my hand. It was just like—like a security blanket," Slater says so sincerely, he sounds believable.

"Hmm, I don't know if I should believe you or not, Slater." Sibley looks him directly in the eyes.

"Well, you've known me my whole life. I might be a rotten kid, but I'm no liar," Slater says with a grin.

"That, I do believe—you are the most rotten kid I've ever met, Slater Hannigan."

"Sibley, I'm really, really sorry I hurt your feelings this year. I just, I'm stupid, what else can I say? I do stupid things, I get in stupid trouble, and I hurt people for stupid reasons. I'm really sorry I caused you so much pain—do you believe me?"

"I'll have to think about it, Slater. Your actions will speak louder than your words. I don't need a new friend, and I especially don't need a new friend out of pity for me, that's for sure. So if you mean what you say, I better see it in action around school, in front of your friends, and in class. You better believe I expect to see a whole new Slater Hannigan, because otherwise I just might tell the whole school and Miss Burbank that I saw writing on your hand for that test. Miss Burbank will never believe you, Slater," Sibley says, standing up tall and finally finding her power to fight back.

"Well, Sibley, I hope Miss Burbank would believe me. She may not, but I know one thing's for sure, I haven't been as awful to her this year as I was last year, and I bet she would at least believe I'm being sincere," Slater says, trying to convince this stubborn girl.

"Well, we shall see," Sibley White says smugly.

"Don't forget, Sibley, I'll tell the whole school it was *you* who wrote my fate on that bag you posted," Slater says, standing just as tall and strong.

"You never heard me confess, so you really have nothing."

"Come on, Sibley, I'm dying to know. How did you know what that witch told me that night?"

"Ugh! Slater, if you must know, I didn't want my parents to know I was leaving a party—once again—before it even got started.

They've been getting on me to be more social and I didn't want the third degree, so I just hid behind some tombstones until the party ended when I knew they would be there to pick me up. I heard the whole thing, and I gotta say, Slater, you looked pretty scared by that witch."

Slater cocks his head sideways to look at Sibley White in a whole new way. This little fraidy cat girl never did go home. Instead she braved the cold and hunger just to spy on everybody else having a good time so that she could pretend in front of her parents that she was one of the cool kids. Who would do that? Somebody who was pretty determined to fit in, that's who.

No wonder Sibley was so mad at Slater for making her feel like an outsider the whole year. He finally got it now.

"Sibley, I really want to tell you again how sorry I am. I guess I am, what you say, the most rotten kid ever. Can I make it up to you?"

"How? I think you're already ahead because you did just save Snickers. I never thanked you for that, did I? Thank you, Slater. I truly don't know what I would have done if you hadn't shown up when you did," Sibley says warmly.

"Well, I know my family is going to the Fourth of July party at Sugar Ridge Park. Do you want to come with us? I'm sure my parents would be cool if I brought another friend," Slater says, extending the first invitation he has ever made to Sibley when he hoped, for real, this time she would say yes.

"I'm not sure. Maybe if my parents come too, or maybe I could just meet you there. I think that might be okay if I'm there with my family," Sibley says, happy to be asked.

"Okay, let's make that call now to my dad's office, and don't worry, Sibley, your other secret about your parents' work is safe with me," Slater says sincerely, extending his hand outwardly as a gesture to shake on it.

Together, Sibley and Slater build a new friendship based on trust that they are each other's secret keepers. Slater never violates her privacy by saying anything to his guy friends about her family, and he never lets on to another living soul that Sibley waited alone in that graveyard until the fun died down. For her part, Sibley lets Slater walk her home for the final three days of school just to be sure those bullies don't return.

When Fourth of July rolls around at Sugar Ridge Park, the entire gang is there: Macaroni and his mother and father; Phil and his father only, since this is his father's weekend for custody; Tobey and his parents; and, of course, Graham and all of his little friends. It is almost like a repeat of the last time they were together at Willow Glenn. But this time will be different, for sure.

While the parents are laughing and sharing memories of when their kids were tots just a short time ago and musing over how they will be starting middle school in another month, nobody seems to be worried about the fact that all of the kids have gone off in their own directions. While little kids play on the swings with their grandparents pushing them from behind, some older kids in high school have taken over the lagoon, riding push boats with girlfriends.

The cackling down below can be heard from high upon the hill where Slater, Tobey, Phil, and Macaroni have escaped. Tucked behind the water tower that hikers use as their turnaround point to head the two miles back down the steep slope, Macaroni is holding court.

"I got them from the mantel above the fireplace," Macaroni says, slowly opening his fist to reveal a strike box filled with matches.

"Dude, at least these aren't all wet like the ones at Willow Glenn," Slater says excitedly.

"What are we gonna light?" Phil asks, wondering if the bunch of leaves he has been pushing together where they have been squatting will be enough.

"We can try leaves, but I don't know how much they smoke. What did the Native Americans use to make smoke signals?" Tobey asks.

"Who can remember any of that history, Tobey?" Slater snaps and takes over the lighting. "Let's try. Ready? Stand back." Slater strikes the first match against the stripe on the outside of the box and *poof* it blows out. "The wind is too strong in this direction. We have to squish together so no air comes through," Slater says as they all huddle more tightly together, shoulder to shoulder.

Swipe, the next match is struck, and this time it is too close to their faces. They all pull back in haste to not get their bangs or their eyebrows singed.

"Ow, that one almost got flickers in my eye, Slater. Watch it," Macaroni says half teasing and half meaning it.

"Dude, you try if you're such an expert," Slater says, clumsily moving back in a little closer, accidentally kicking through the leaf pile Phil is now complaining about wanting to light.

"Oh, I want a stick, not leaves. Maybe we can light a stick on fire like the cavemen," Macaroni says.

"That would be so cool—where are the sticks?" Slater says to the rest of the guys as they look through the long dried grass blowing in the wind and kick at pebbles on the gravel road that stirs up dust with every stub of the toe.

"Okay, no sticks. I guess that makes sense since there're no trees around here," Slater says, pointing out the obvious. "All right then, let's use Phil's leaves. Everybody push 'em together again."

As the boys hover around, squatting down low like sitting ducks, the last lucky strike of the match will be their unluckiest one of all. This one produces a flame—and yes, those leaves do burn. In all of their excitement to see that they have made fire like the caveman, they have forgotten how fast a flame can spread. Somehow, the dried grass three feet away seemed too far to reach, but what they did not count on was the wind picking up, scattering those leaves every which way.

"Slaaaater, put it out, put it out!" Macaroni screams.

"Everybody, start stomping!" Slater shouts.

"Oh, man, ouch!" Tobey screams in a panic as the sparks ricochet off of his leg.

"Phil, we gotta run! Guys, we gotta go! The hill's burning, let's go!" Slater yells as he looks around at the small patch of fire that seems to be chasing its way up the hill to touch every dry blade of grass as fast as the wind can shift directions.

The boys hightail it out of there, hoping they can make it back to their families before anyone realizes they have been gone for too long. At the bottom of the hill, they make a plan to each go to their own house, take a shower to get the dust and the smoke off of them, and then get back to the park, which is only two blocks away from their neighborhood. They cross the street and see what all of the families in the park are pointing to now: smoke—lots and lots of smoke.

They disband, but at the sight of frantic parents calling out for them, they know there will never be time enough to get home and back. So they do the next logical thing. Each of them jumps into the lagoon that is not meant for swimmers, but at least they can hide the smell of smoke and sulfur. When they get out of the water, they try to act casual while families scurry to pick up their blankets and cart out their baskets at the sound of sirens wailing from a half mile away.

As soon as Macaroni comes out of the water, his mother runs toward him, grabbing the back of his wet shirt and moving him swiftly to the car.

After Phil's father finds him at the opposite end of the park and Tobey reunites with his parents, Slater comes out of the water to see a pair of eyes locked on him that makes him want to disappear. More than any birthday candle wish he could make for the next thousand years, he wishes Sibley White was not standing here right now.

Sibley White stares at Slater and this odd combination of four boys who suddenly jump into the lagoon for an unplanned swim—with all of their clothes on. It makes little sense to her unless, of course, she has just discovered one more incriminating secret about her new friend—this one too big for her to keep.

FROM THE AUTHOR

Thank you, dear reader, for burning through these pages of *Mischief* with Slater Hannigan and his friends. Here is a sneak peek at what lies ahead for the gang in the next book called *Mayhem—Stefania Shaffer*

CHAPTER 1
Somebody's In Trouble

Whirr, whirr, whirrrr sounds the siren as it wails from a mile away. Its screaming rhythm does not seem unusual—nothing for parents to pay much attention to anyway—until they hear the full throttle bellow of the final alto horn. Its lingering echo blares from many blocks away still, but its signal warns the crowd—I am coming.

At first, the families of Everly stop their chewing in order to listen more intently. The hot dogs and cobs of corn are now suspended in midair as everyone freezes. Maybe the danger is headed in *another* direction, toward *another* grand park, where *other* families will meet its fate instead. Maybe it's a false alarm, they hope, as they wait for the nerve-jangling sounds tormenting them now to come to an abrupt halt so they may continue with their celebration as planned.

While families at other parks farther away listen to the same ear-piercing roar, wondering the same awful thoughts, *they* will breathe the collective sigh of relief when the threat of emergency tucks itself around the corner, fading into the distance toward its intended destination—the grand Sugar Ridge Park.

When the first fire engine blasts into the west end parking lot entrance—followed by a second manned by four firefighters—parents exchange befuddled looks with one another, trying to figure out what the matter could be. Curious expressions stretching between them, they watch intently as the firefighter in charge directs the second Engine to drive around back using the fire lane—pointing with his big oven mitt gloves made of fire retardant grey cloth to where the danger has started.

Fathers and mothers turn their heads slowly as their gazes move with the firefighters' fingers still waving toward the eastern edge of Sugar Ridge Park where the hill behind them has caught ablaze. It does not seem to make sense yet because from two acres away, they can see nothing clearly. But, it must be *something* because the roaring engine of a third truck rounds the corner now—its ladder and basket ready to shoot water from extreme heights.

"There it is! I see it, Dad! It's a fire!" Graham squeals loudly. As soon as he does, the other kids move to where Graham stands so they can also get the best view. Sure enough, a lick of orange tickles the blue horizon, and a plume of black smoke fills the sky. A bullhorn carries the urgent instructions from the battalion chief. "Families, we need for you to clear the park. Please don't run. You have plenty of time, but we ask you to take your children and gather what you can of your picnic items, swiftly. You have only a few minutes to evacuate this area. Sheriffs will be filing you out of the parking lot in an orderly fashion so we can maintain your safety."

Chief Reynolds has seen this a thousand times. Every Fourth of July, his worry about unintended fires increases year to year. This season has been especially dry, causing high alert status for off-duty firefighters who might need to be called in to help battle a raging fire that has spread out of control. The ban on fireworks usually limits the prospect of fire danger, but until Chief Reynolds does some investigating, he won't have the answers for the only two questions he cares about—*what* caused this and *who* is behind it?

In the few minutes it has taken to disrupt the sense of security families have been enjoying at their annual neighborhood Fourth of July picnic, another kind of alarm cries more loudly than the horns heard on Engine 44.

"Where is he, Hank?" Lynn Hannigan shouts urgently across the length of eight picnic tables to her husband gathered with his golf buddies in one of the beautiful gazebos.

"Lynn, not here," Hank Hannigan screams back as he motions for her to come closer.

Frantically, Lynn moves in. She grabs her youngest son, Graham, by the elbow, clumsily dragging him beside her as his feet practically hover over the turf beneath him. He half wriggles from her grip, but his strides fail to keep pace with hers.

"Graham, stay right with me, and I don't want to hear a sound out of you," Lynn says in full mama-bear mode. She bolts halfway across the park in what seems like ten long paces. She is not even out of breath, but the sweat drenching her thin T-shirt beneath her armpits and down her back indicates that she is hot.

However, the temperatures of the sweltering heat on this July 4th and the dozens of barbecue grills she has been artfully dodging— while keeping ahold of the only son she *can* find at the moment—are not what has her steaming. It is the smoke from the hill fire behind the park that has her worried her soon-to-be sixth-grade son Slater might know something about this.

"Mom, your fingernails are gouging into my arm, ouch!" Graham says in full protest. "I'm not a baby. I can walk by myself," he finishes, trying to release himself from his mother's claws.

"Graham, I mean it. Not one word until we find Slater," Lynn says sharply.

꒬ ꒬ ꒬ ꒬

Knock, knock. Thrump, thrump. "Who is it?" a small voice calls from behind the heavy wooden front door.

"Police officers. We'd like to speak with you."

A chain wriggles from its placeholder across the door. The sound of a deadbolt untwisting sends a loud click through the entryway. The doorknob jiggles slightly before turning and then pulls away from its jam with a jarring struggle. "Sorry, the door sticks," come the words, soft-spoken and friendly. Eyes that peer out from behind the door with the body still out of sight seem warm, yet uninviting. "May I help you?"

"Yes, ma'am, we are going door-to-door to ask the neighbors if they might know something about how today's fire got started. Is it all right if we come in and speak with you for a few minutes? You were at the Fourth of July picnic today at Sugar Ridge Park, right?" the first officer asks innocently. It is, after all, the fortieth house he has stopped by this afternoon.

"Yes, I was at the park, officer," she states simply.

"If we can just take a few moments of your time, we'd like to ask you a couple of routine questions. You were there at the time the fire broke out?"

"Yes, officer—"

A voice calls down from one of the rooms upstairs, "Sibley, who is at the door?"

"Mother, it's police officers asking about the fire," Sibley hollers back urgently.

Halfway through her explanation, Sibley's mother navigates her way down the staircase. Her hair is disheveled, her apron is soiled, and she quickly removes her rubber gloves.

"Officers, so sorry to keep you waiting at the door. Please, won't you come in?"

As Mrs. White shows the officers to her living room, Sibley White stares longingly at the street looking for someone she might know. Alas, nobody there—Sibley White is all on her own.

Dear Reader,

Did you enjoy Mischief? Is your heart still racing? Are you wondering what will happen to our fine friends in the next book? Oh, it is delicious. But I am sworn to secrecy.

But *you* don't have to keep Mischief a secret from the world. In fact, would you be willing to go straight to amazon.com to write an honest review for the author? She is competing against all of those other books you read and is hoping to get your friends interested in reading all about Slater, Macaroni, and, of course, me.

It's pretty easy. Just go to: www.amazon.com and then type in Stefania Shaffer.

Find the book, write a review, add some stars and then, snap, you're done.

As for me, I have already cleared a special spot on my shelf for all four of the new books in the Mischief series. See you in the V.I.P. Club!

Yours truly,
Sibley White

P.S. To become a V.I.P. member of the Mischief-Makers Club sign up for my newsletter at www.MischiefSeries.com.

You will be first to find top-secret giveaways and previews of new releases from future books.

Kids visit: www.MischiefSeries.com

Parents visit: www.StefaniaShaffer.com

All books by Stefania Shaffer

Fiction for Middle Grade readers:

Heroes Don't Always Wear Capes
Mischief Series: Mischief-Book 1
Mischief Series: Mayhem-Book 2
Mischief Series: Menace-Book 3
Mischief Series: Malice-Book 4

Non-Fiction for Adults:

9 Realities of Caring for an Elderly Parent: A Love Story of a Different Kind, a memoir

9 Realities of Caring for an Elderly Parent: The Companion Play-book, accompanying workbook